His
Keeper

KATHRYN BELLAMY

Heartline
Books

KATHRYN BELLAMY

Kathryn Bellamy was born in Lincolnshire, one of the most beautiful cathedral cities in England, and still lives there. She was educated at Queen Elizabeth grammar School in Horncastle, Lincolnshire and, after gaining excellent examination results, went to work in a Bank.

A number of part-time jobs followed which left Kathryn free to concentrate on what she enjoys most – writing, and *reading*, romantic fiction. Amongst her favourite authors are Jilly Cooper and Rosemary Rogers and Kathryn admits to a secret passion for bodice rippers!

In her spare time she enjoys reading, tennis and yoga. But perhaps Kathryn's most challenging pastime at the moment is going on safari to the bottom of her garden – where she never knows what she might find, as recent visitors have included snakes and giant toads!

chapter one

'More flowers for you, Chrissie,' announced Sally, stifling a sigh of disappointment as she handed over the large bouquet which had just been delivered to the estate agency where both girls worked.

'Oh, God,' Chrissie groaned, unimpressed. Red roses. Again, she thought ungratefully.

'Yeah, you poor thing. Imagine receiving daily bouquets from one of the most eligible bachelors in town. It must be dreadful for you,' Sally said, her voice dripping with sarcasm and thinly-veiled jealousy. Chrissie shrugged.

'He's only doing it to try and get me into bed.'

'I repeat; you poor thing…' Sally began. Grinning, Chrissie put up a hand to silence her.

'Ben Fairfax is drop-dead gorgeous and full of surface charm, I grant you,' she acknowledged: after all, that was what had first attracted her to him. 'But he is also spoilt and immature.'

'He's older than you,' Sally pointed out.

'He's still immature.' Chrissie hesitated, then confided, 'I'm going to tell him I don't want to go out with him any more.'

'Really? I think you're crazy. You can certainly point him in my direction,' Sally said, but without much hope that he would be interested. Unlike tall, slender, blonde Chrissie, she was short, plumpish and mousy. Her one attempt at dying her hair blonde had been a disaster – she had ended up looking like a punk rocker, with vivid green streaks – frizzy green streaks, at that.

'With pleasure,' Chrissie agreed. Ben was simply becoming too pushy about sex and her refusals, at first accepted good-naturedly, were now increasingly met with bad temper and a fit of childish sulks which he assumed would be instantly forgiven after he made a phone call to the florist.

'When did you decide to finish with him?'

'Oh, I guess I've been thinking about it for the past week. But it's his birthday today, and he's having a party with all his friends, so I'll wait until tomorrow to tell him. If I'm lucky, he'll go off with another girl tonight and save me the bother,' she added, dreading the scene Ben might make. It was obvious to Chrissie that very few people had ever said 'no' to Ben Fairfax. The one exception seemed to be his older brother, Trent, whom Ben glumly referred to as Torquemada.

'Would you like these?' Chrissie tossed the roses over to Sally's desk. 'I'm running out of vases.'

'OK, thanks!' Sally brightened, already planning to tell her flatmate that they were from an admirer. Which of course they were, only not from one of her own. Still, why spoil a good story with minor details?

Chrissie glanced around to check the manager wasn't within earshot, then dialled Ben's mobile number. He sounded out of breath when he answered, and her brows rose speculatively. Had he already moved on to someone more co-operative than she was? She sincerely hoped so.

'I just wanted to say thank you for the flowers,' she said, scowling when Sally hooted loudly in derision. 'And to wish you happy birthday,' she paused; he was still breathing heavily. 'Where are you?'

'At the gym, I'm playing squash,' he explained.

'Oh.' Chrissie felt disappointment rather than a shred of relief that she hadn't caught him in bed with some other girl. Proof, if she still needed any, that she was right to end the relationship. 'Listen, Ben, don't come and pick me up this evening, I'll make my own way to the pub,' she said. And my own way back home, alone, she added silently.

'Why?'

'Um, I have to escort a couple around a house late this afternoon and I might not have time to go home and change,' she explained.

'Liar!' Sally said loudly. Chrissie reached over to pick up the roses and pretended to hit her around the head with them.

'OK,' Ben apparently hadn't heard Sally's interjection. 'You'll definitely come, though, won't you?' He sounded anxious and Chrissie bit her lip: ending relationships had never been easy for her and she had a feeling that Ben was going to be harder than most to shake off.

'Of course. The Royal Oak, eight o'clock. I'll be there,' she promised.

'Great! I've got a surprise for you, sweetie,' he said happily before disconnecting.

'Great,' Chrissie echoed hollowly as she replaced the receiver. She looked across at Sally. 'He says he's got a surprise for me,' she told her. Sally grinned.

'Yeah, and no prizes for guessing what that is!'

'Oh, shut up,' Chrissie muttered.

Chrissie slotted her second-hand Mini into a parking space outside the Royal Oak shortly after eight o clock that evening. As she clambered out and locked it she noted that many of Ben's crowd had already arrived; her car was definitely the poor relation amongst the gleaming array of Porsches, BMWs and other sporty numbers which she couldn't name but which were obviously expensive.

'I'll give you a polish at the weekend,' she promised her Mini, then took a deep breath to steady her nerves before entering the fray.

She didn't know Ben's friends very well, but had found them difficult to like. They seemed to her to be a rather shallow group, concerned only with the next party or holiday. None of them had to work for a living and she had gained the impression that they rather looked down on anyone less privileged than themselves.

Chrissie had deliberately dressed very simply for the evening, in a plain blue shift dress and very little make-up, and had tied her hair back into a ponytail. Even if she had wanted to, there was no way she could compete with the other girls' designer frocks, and tonight she definitely didn't mind if the others outshone her and caught Ben's attention.

'Chrissie!' Ben spotted her as soon as she entered the bar and began making his way over to her. She noticed, with dismay, that he was already unsteady on his feet and guessed he had been drinking for most of the afternoon. At least his Porsche wasn't one of those she had seen outside, so he didn't intend driving.

'Happy Birthday,' she kissed his cheek and handed over the card and wrapped CDs she had bought him.

'Thanks, sweetie,' Ben aimed for but missed her mouth, and instead nuzzled her neck as he slung a strong arm around her waist and drew her over to meet his friends.

'Hi, Chrissie. Good to see you again.' The friendly greetings were mostly from the men; the girls eyed her plain frock and exchanged 'what does he see in her?' glances.

'I say, your surname's Brennan, isn't it?' Gareth asked her. Are you related to Gus and Ophelia Brennan? I met them at the golf club recently.'

'Sorry, I've never heard of them,' Chrissie smiled at him, knowing he was trying to be nice. She had once overheard him berating his girlfriend for describing Chrissie as 'a nobody from nowhere'.

'You are from Farminster, though, aren't you?' he persisted.

'Yes, born and bred, but I don't have any family here now. I'm an only child and my parents died some years ago,' she told him.

'But you're only a baby now!' he smiled sympathetically. 'How did you manage alone?'

'I was taken into care until I finished school and then I got a job.' She faced him squarely. 'Lots of people do, you know,' she couldn't resist adding.

'You were in care?' Ben put in, looking shocked. 'I didn't know that – I assumed you had grandparents or aunts and uncles to look after you.'

'Did you? Would it have put you off me if you'd known? After all, everyone knows kids in care are trouble with a capital T. The boys are all joy-riders and the girls shoplifting sluts!' she said bitterly, the words tumbling out of their own volition, startling her as much as anyone else.

It was a long time since she had felt the need to defend herself against the prejudice often felt towards children in care. Maybe this wealthy, overprivileged crowd were making her feel inferior, which was rubbish. She realized she was shaking violently and snatched the glass of wine Ben silently handed to her, gulping it down before remembering that she had to drive home.

'Of course it wouldn't have put me off,' Ben said softly,

kindly, his gaze warm and concerned for her obvious distress, and Chrissie suddenly recalled why she had been attracted to him when she'd first met him. His carefree attitude to life and even his immaturity had been endearing in a way; even the death of his father had affected him very little, or so he had claimed. He had been happy at his boarding school and it had been his older brother who'd had to deal with the funeral and try to comfort their mother. Ben had been shielded as much as possible and every effort made to ensure that his life continued as before.

Even now he received an income from his brother despite Trent's constant complaints that he failed to carry out the duties he was supposed to, duties which entailed helping to manage the family estate here in Farminster while Trent dealt with the Fairfax property company based in London.

Such regular complaints from an employer would have resulted in redundancy for most people, but not for Ben. And, after all, it was having to worry about paying the mortgage or rent which propelled most young people into adulthood. Ben had no such worries; he lived in a luxurious barn conversion in the grounds of Fairfax Hall.

'In fact,' Ben continued, his arm still holding her close to him, 'I want to show you, show everyone' – and in an expansive gesture, he flung out the other arm, which unfortunately held a full glass of whisky, thereby showering half a dozen people nearby in neat Scotch – 'how much I want to take care of you.' Chrissie wished she'd kept her mouth shut.

'I don't need taking care of…' she began.

'Course you do, sweetie. I told you I had a surprise for you, didn't I?' he beamed at her and Chrissie smiled weakly back. What was he on about? 'Everybody! Listen!' Ben yelled and the room became as quiet as it was possible for a crowded pub to be. 'I want you all to hear this,' he said. He turned to Chrissie and, to her horror, dropped to one knee while fumbling in his breast pocket. Oh God, oh no, please let it not be a ring she prayed fervently. But it was – a huge rock of an emerald and Chrissie recoiled from it as if it had been cursed.

She glanced wildly around, hoping no-one had noticed. The noise level had risen again but many people were watching. She hoped they were too drunk to remember this in the morning. In fact, she hoped Ben was too drunk to remember it! And the prospect of getting drunk herself was becoming more tempting with every passing second. How had she got herself into this? And, more to the point, how did she get herself out of it without hurting and humiliating Ben?

'Don't do this, Ben!' she hissed. 'Tell everyone it's a joke! And stand up!'

'Can't stand up,' he grinned at her. 'I'm drunk with happiness!'

'Not to mention a bottle of Scotch,' sniffed a haughty blonde dressed in what appeared to be her underwear. Scraps of red lace barely covered her assets and Chrissie side-stepped deliberately so that Ben would get an eyeful of Miss Sex-on-legs. Annabel-Somebody-or-Other, she thought vaguely; it had occurred to her before that the other girl was jealous. Unfortunately for both girls, Ben only had eyes – albeit bloodshot and badly focused – for Chrissie.

'Chrissie, sweetie,' he grabbed the hand she had snatched away and tried to place the ring on her finger. Chrissie hastily curled her fingers into her palm. 'Will you do me the honour…'

'Don't, Ben. Not here,' she pleaded.

'You wanna go somewhere private?' His eyes lit up at the prospect of finally luring her into bed.

'No!'

'Oh, OK; I'm probably too drunk anyway; been drinking all afternoon,' he said, as if she hadn't already guessed that! 'Getting up the nerve to propose,' he added, and gave a lopsided grin that tore at her heart. He was an idiot, but he was a loveable idiot.

'Oh, Ben,' she said despairingly. All he really wanted was to sleep with her – if she'd done so, he would never have come up with this crazy notion of marriage, she was sure of that. She wasn't worried that her refusal would break his heart, or even dent it, but he would be terribly embarrassed if she rejected him in front of his friends. 'We'll discuss this tomorrow,' she prevaricated.

'Put the ring on,' Ben insisted.

'Oh, very well,' Chrissie decided to end the scene as quickly as possible and allowed him to slide the ring on to her finger. 'It's much too big,' she said, vastly relieved to have an excuse not to wear it. 'Here, put it back in your pocket – I should hate to lose it.' She shoved the wretched thing back into his jacket pocket.

She looked around to check how many people had witnessed the ridiculous proposal and, although a couple of his friends whooped and slapped his back in congratulation, they seemed as drunk as Ben and would hopefully have only a hazy memory of it in the morning. Ben would be able to pass it off as a joke, she thought optimistically.

Fortunately for her, all attention was quickly diverted away from them when a uniformed WPC strode in, pretended to arrest Ben for being in charge of a golf buggy whilst drunk, then switched on a portable cassette recorder and proceeded to perform a striptease. Great timing, Chrissie thought gladly, and she wasn't referring to the stripper's provocative movements!

'I'm just going to the loo,' she whispered to Ben, who nodded but didn't take his eyes off the WPC, who had just whipped off her skirt to reveal stockings and suspenders. As Chrissie left the room, she saw Ben willingly hold out his wrists to be handcuffed, much to the delight of his friends. Terrific! The proposal definitely wouldn't prove to be the most memorable part of the evening!

She locked herself in a cubicle and sat there for a while, listening to the crescendo of noise as the stripper presumably rid herself of her underwear, and wondered if it would be cowardly of her to go home now without another word to Ben. Reluctantly, she decided it would and, sighing, left her sanctuary.

The blonde, Annabel, wearing an excuse for a bikini and possibly annoyed that she was being outshone by someone wearing even less, was in the cloakroom, re-applying scarlet lip gloss. She glanced at Chrissie in the mirror.

'Have you met Ben's family yet?'

'No.'

'Thought not.' Scarlet lips thinned. 'His mother's a darling, mad as a hatter, of course, but very sweet. Trent, however… well, you'll see,' she smiled slightly. Chrissie was too irritated by her superior attitude to explain that she had no intention of meeting Ben's family, nor had any reason to.

'I'm sure I shall,' she said instead, and swept out, head held high.

Back in the bar, she discovered that the stripper had finished her act and already left. Ben was involved in some kind of drinking competition with three of his friends; amid much laughter, they were taking it in turns to recite tongue-twisters and rewarding themselves with another drink, whether or not they pronounced them correctly.

She quickly realized that she wouldn't be missed if she left. Feeling rather furtive, she hovered on the fringes of the crowd for a few minutes while gradually edging backwards towards the door. With one final look back over her shoulder she turned and almost ran, gulping in the fresh air of freedom as she dashed across the car park.

She didn't feel totally safe until she was in the Mini and heading for home. God, what a nightmare! Still, her one consolation was that they were all so plastered they probably wouldn't remember a thing when they sobered up.

'So, how was the party?' Sally asked, next morning.

'Bloody awful!' Chrissie shuddered; she'd suffered nightmares throughout the night. 'He proposed. Well, sort of. He was very drunk.'

'Proposed? What did you say?'

'Not a lot. What could I say, in front of his friends? I'm going to phone him later and ask him to meet me for lunch and get it sorted out.' But when she finally got through to Ben on his mobile, he was in his car headed for London.

'Sorry, sweetie; it'll have to wait until tonight – I've been summoned by Torquemada,' he told her, referring to his older brother. 'This line's terrible – did you hear me?'

'Just about,' Chrissie stuck a finger in her other ear. 'We really do need to…talk,' she sighed, as the connection broke abruptly. She re-dialled several times throughout the morning, but without success. The battery must be dead. She resigned herself to waiting until he contacted her, but the delay made her extremely nervous.

Trent Fairfax sighed heavily when Ben, unshaven, unkempt and obviously hungover, sauntered into his office. Sometimes he felt as if he were Ben's father, not his brother. And the feeling didn't lessen as the years passed, either.

Trent had been twenty two, Ben only thirteen, when their father had unexpectedly died of a massive heart attack. Trent had been enjoying life at university but, when it became apparent that his mother couldn't cope alone with her grief, he had abandoned his studies to take over running the rather diverse family affairs, which ranged from their farming interests in Farminster to property development throughout the south east.

He had wisely kept on his father's most experienced staff, retaining the Board of Directors and keeping on the estate manager. He had listened and learned, and over the past ten years the family businesses had prospered. Ben, however, Trent thought sourly, seemed to imagine that all Trent's hard work had been solely for his young brother's benefit. When, after finishing school, Ben had said he would like to attend Agricultural College, Trent had been delighted, hopeful that he would eventually be able to leave the running of the estate farms to his brother. However, Ben took his responsibilities so lightly that Trent hadn't yet felt able to dispense with the services of his estate manager.

'Why didn't you tell me you wanted to take Grandmother's ring out of the bank?' he demanded, without preamble. 'I had to hear it from Chambers – he was in a helluva state when he realised it shouldn't have been released without my permission.'

'It was left to me in her will,' Ben said sulkily. Trent always made him feel as if he were about ten years old. 'It's my ring.'

'Not until you're twenty-five,' Trent reminded him. 'Why do you want it? I sincerely hope you haven't sold it,' he said, his blue eyes narrowed in suspicion. Dark-haired and blue-eyed, there was a definite resemblance between the two brothers, but Trent's features were harsher, his face leaner, with a tautness about his mouth and jaw that warned he was not a man to cross swords with.

'Of course I haven't sold it!' Ben was indignant. 'I…I've got engaged.'

'You've *what*?'

'Got engaged. To be married,' Ben clarified. Trent frowned darkly; this was the last thing he had expected to hear. Then a slight smile played around his mouth and his features lightened, lifting the years.

'She won't sleep with you,' he guessed, his grin broadening as he noted his brother's discomfiture. Ben stared stonily ahead, refusing to admit defeat and stayed silent. 'Hmm, is she virtuous?' Trent mused. 'Or perhaps just very clever, holding out until she gets a ring on her finger. Who is she? Do I know her?'

'I doubt it. She lives in Farminster but doesn't hang around with my crowd. Her name's Chrissie, and she's adorable,' Ben told him dreamily.

'I'm sure she is,' Trent agreed dryly. 'How long have you known her?' He was quite amused by this turn of events: when the bank manager had phoned, he had assumed that Ben was once again short of cash. He knew his little brother well enough to be sure this romance would quickly founder, as had so many others before it. However, so far as Trent was aware, Ben had never actually proposed before, so he decided to pay a little more attention than he normally would have done.

'Only a few weeks,' Ben admitted. 'But I fell for her straight away. She's different, she…'

'Where did you meet?' Trent interrupted, having neither the time nor the inclination to hear the undoubtedly long list of her attributes.

'I almost knocked her over in the Porsche,' Ben admitted, shame-faced. 'She twisted her ankle trying to get out of my way so I gave her a lift back to work.'

'She works? That's an improvement on your usual girl-friends,' Trent commented dryly. 'What does she do?'

'She's with Thomson and Wilson, the estate agents in Market Street.'

'I know them, I'm considering doing business with them over that new estate off Tanner Lane,' Trent told him, then returned to the main reason for the meeting. 'You'll have to ask her to return the ring, I'm afraid. Buy her another out of your allowance, if you must, but explain that the emerald isn't yours to give,' he instructed. Ben scowled.

'I can't ask for it back,' he protested.

'If you don't, I will,' Trent assured him grimly. 'If she loves you, she'll understand,' he added mockingly, quite unable to take this 'love' affair seriously.

Ben stared at him mulishly: how could he ask Chrissie to hand it back? He had only a hazy memory of proposing but had the distinct feeling she had not been exactly thrilled by the public spectacle. He supposed he had done it all wrong; should have taken her to an expensive restaurant, just the two of them, and popped the question in a romantic, candle-lit setting. And now Trent wanted, no, was ordering him to get the ring back.

Ben fought down the sudden, impotent rage that engulfed him; rage at his grandparents and his father for

trusting everything to Trent and nothing to him, rage at
Trent for continuing to hang on to the family purse strings
and doling out an allowance as if he, Ben, were still a
schoolboy.

However, he knew Trent wouldn't hesitate to cut off his
cash flow if he disobeyed him. Ben rubbed his aching
head and tried to think. Hadn't Chrissie said the ring was
too big for her? Perhaps he could ask for its return on the
pretext of altering the size, have a cheap copy made and
hand the original back to Trent?

He brightened at the brilliance of that idea and managed
a smile for his brother. Not too much of a smile, though,
since Trent was suspicious to the point of paranoia!

'OK – you're the boss,' he said, with deliberate reluctance. Trent nodded.

'Don't you forget it. I think I'll come down to Farminster this weekend; I'd like to meet…er…?'

'Chrissie. Brennan,' Ben supplied.

'Has Ma met her yet?'

'No.'

'Bring her over to dinner on Saturday evening.' It was
an order rather than a suggestion, and again Ben had to
hide his irritation. His plans for Chrissie on Saturday night
had *not* included his mother and brother!

'I'll ask Chrissie,' he said. 'May I go now? Is the lecture
over?'

'Not quite,' Trent frowned at his tone. 'Did you drive
here or take the train?'

'I drove.'

'You look hungover to me. I suggest you crash out for
a few hours before driving back. You can use my flat –
the cleaner's there today; I'll phone her and get her to
make up the bed in the spare room.'

'Thanks,' Ben nodded; he really did feel knackered.

Trent forgot about Ben and his no doubt short-term fiancée for several hours. It was only when he rang his mother to tell her that he'd be home for the weekend, that something she said struck a chord of memory. She was prattling on about an old friend of his father, James Hawksworth.

'Ma,' he cut her gossip short. 'Hawksworth's son – Charles? Wasn't he involved with a local girl some years ago before James packed him off to Australia to get him out of her clutches?

'Yes, that's right. Fancy you remembering that! Charles was besotted with her…now, what was her name?' she wondered out loud. Trent didn't enlighten her, but he knew: Christina Brennan.

He cut the conversation short and sat back in his leather chair, swivelling around to gaze unseeingly out of the window at the London skyline. Ben's infatuation had become a serious matter. He had been joking when he'd enquired whether Chrissie was virtuous or clever in not going to bed with Ben. Now he knew the answer; she was astute, no doubt teasing and promising, but always stopping short of making love, hinting that she wasn't interested in sex without commitment.

Charles Hawksworth would inherit a fortune when his father died, as would Ben in another year. It could hardly be a coincidence that Christina Brennan had caught the eye of the two wealthiest young men in the district. His mouth tightened; Miss Brennan would soon realize that, in him, she was no longer dealing with a hormonally-driven youth with more money than sense!

chapter two

Ben slept away the rest of the afternoon but, anxious to be gone before Trent returned home and find something else to lecture him about, arranged for a wake-up call and left the flat before six.

The rush hour traffic hindered him and, despite being anxious to see Chrissie, he stopped off at a motorway service area for food and coffee. The battery in his mobile was flat, so he phoned her from there, to say he was on his way back to Farminster.

'Ben! I've been trying to contact you all day!' she exclaimed crossly. Ben chose to ignore her tone of voice.

'Have you missed me?'

'No! Ben I really wish you hadn't made a fool of yourself – and me – last night…'

'I asked you to marry me,' he retorted, stung. 'How is that making a fool of either of us?'

'You were drunk. And it isn't the sort of thing to do in public, because,' she hesitated, then plunged on: she simply couldn't wait any more, her nerves were in tatters! 'The answer's "no", Ben.' Then she said more gently, 'That's why I wish you had proposed privately. If you had, no one else need ever have known about it.'

There was a stunned silence. 'But you can't have changed your mind,' he said, bewildered and trying to remember whether he had done something that he shouldn't at the party. He only had a hazy memory of events after around nine o'clock.

'I haven't changed my mind. I never said "yes" Ben,' Chrissie said patiently. 'Come on, admit it, you don't want to marry me, you only want to get me into bed.' Ben decided to ignore that, too.

'I've told Trent we're engaged,' he said, as if that clinched it. Chrissie sighed.

'Then tell him we're un-engaged!' she retorted. 'I'm sorry, Ben, perhaps I should have made it clear last night, but I didn't want to humiliate you in front of your friends.'

'Didn't want to humiliate me?' he repeated incredulously. 'I suppose you imagine it won't be embarrassing for me to explain why you changed your mind within the space of twenty-four hours!' His voice dripped sarcasm, but there was underlying pain, too, and Chrissie sighed. She hadn't expected it to be this difficult.

'I told you, I haven't changed my mind – I never intended marrying you. I'm sorry.'

'This doesn't make any sense – you're obviously overwrought,' he said and Chrissie had to bite back a peal of hysterical laughter. Next, he'd be blaming her intransigence on premenstrual tension! 'I'm coming straight over to see you.'

'No! I won't be here; I'm going out,' she fibbed. There was nothing to be gained by going over and over the same ground.

'Out? Who with?' he demanded.

'That's none of your business, Ben. I don't want to see you tonight. In fact, it's probably better if we don't see each other again.'

'Who the hell do you think you are?' For the first time in their relationship, the innate arrogance of the upper class was very evident; that inbred knowledge of superiority which came from generations of being Lords of the Manor. 'I won't let you do this to me.'

'There's nothing you can do, Ben.' Chrissie was suddenly weary and depressed. She really had enjoyed his friendship over the past few weeks but now that too was over. 'Goodbye.'

'You low-class frigid little bitch!' Ben slammed the handset down so hard he thought he must have broken a bone in his hand. He swore fluently, strode out to the car park, stopped, hesitated, and turned round to go and phone her back, his quick temper already cooling. That last remark had been well out of order, he acknowledged uncomfortably.

He found more coins and re-dialled Chrissie's number, but she didn't pick up – either she'd already gone out or she was refusing to speak to him. He let it ring for five minutes, then, anger bubbling to the surface again, went back to his car. He gunned the Porsche into tyre-squealing life and tore out on to the motorway, overtaking slower vehicles and settling into the fast lane at ninety miles an hour.

Fumbling for a CD, he failed to notice that the car in front was travelling somewhat slower than his own. Almost too late, he glanced up at the road ahead, slammed his foot on the brake and swerved to avoid a collision, narrowly missing the crash barrier of the central reservation before straightening the Porsche.

Whew! That had been close. He gave a one-fingered salute to the blameless driver he'd almost crashed into, but slowed his own speed and concentrated on his driving. But he was still angry, hurt and preoccupied, and the bad headache from the previous night's drinking and lack of sleep hadn't abated much. His luck ran out when he was only three miles from home and had relaxed a little too much on the familiar roads; he misjudged a bend, the Porsche left the road at speed and ploughed into a fence before flipping over on to its roof.

Chrissie was relieved when the evening passed without further phone calls or a furious hammering at her front door. His parting shot had both hurt and angered her and, although she guessed it was Ben who had tried to call immediately after the insult, presumably to apologise, she was in no mood to forgive him, or to continue with the pointless conversation. God, he'd got a nerve! She had spent the last month fending off his advances – how dare he accuse her of egging him on?

She didn't sleep at all well, re-living the quarrel and half expecting him to turn up on the doorstep. Ben kept very late hours and had absolutely no conception of anyone having to be up early to go to work. Several times he had phoned her at two or three in the morning, simply to chat or to invite her out the following day.

Despite being undisturbed, Chrissie felt heavy-eyed and lethargic as she prepared for the office; even a cold shower and several cups of hot coffee failed to wake her totally, and she felt distinctly out of sorts as she drove into the town centre.

'You look rough,' Sally commented: she and the manager, Reg Ford, were already opening the mail when Chrissie pushed open the door. Reg glanced meaningfully at his watch and then at Chrissie. She repeated the gesture and glared at him. She knew she was exactly one minute late. Creep.

'Thanks a lot and good morning to you, too,' she responded to Sally. 'I had a bad night.' She paused, wanting to confide in Sally but not while Reg Ford's ears were flapping. There was a foolproof way to get rid of him, though. 'I started my period,' she said and, sure enough, the manager disappeared at the speed of light at the mere mention of 'women's problems'. The two girls grinned conspiratorially at Reg's retreating back, but waited until he closed the door of his private office behind him before speaking.

'Ben?' Sally guessed.

'Mm, I had to tell him over the phone that I don't want to marry him. He wasn't best pleased; in fact, he was quite nasty and said I'd been leading him on.' She couldn't repeat the actual phrase Ben had used. 'So I told him I didn't want to see him again, and he didn't like that, either! Then he said he was coming to see me, although I made it clear I didn't want him to. I was on tenterhooks all night.'

'Did he turn up?'

'No.'

'Maybe he'll back off, now.'

'I hope so,' Chrissie said fervently.

'Or maybe he'll send more red roses!'

'You're a great help,' Chrissie muttered. However, she was soon to wish red roses were her only problem…

Shortly before eleven, Trent Fairfax pushed open the door and walked in. Sally was sitting nearest the door and his glance flickered over her, briefly and dismissively, before settling on Chrissie, who was updating the rows of sales brochures.

Leggy blondes had always been Ben's weakness, and this one was a beauty, he thought dispassionately. To add to the obvious physical attributes there was a disturbing air of fragility and vulnerability, heightened by a rather haunting look in the depths of large dark blue, almost violet eyes. She probably practises that demeanour in front of the mirror, he thought cynically; a carefully cultivated air designed to ensnare gullible young fools such as Charles Hawksworth and, latterly, Ben.

Chrissie became aware of the man's scrutiny and lifted her head to return his gaze. He was tall and broad-shouldered, the cashmere sweater he was wearing over dark slacks moulded a powerfully-muscled frame. His hair was black, cut short and with a sprinkling of grey at the temples and his face, too harsh to be described as handsome, was nevertheless compelling, with piercingly bright blue eyes which seemed to miss nothing. Their brilliance contrasted sharply with the shadowed circles beneath them and the hollows in his cheeks.

He looks as if he had as little sleep as I did, Chrissie found herself thinking, but, in his case she suspected, not for just the one night.

The wonderful sapphire eyes narrowed as he raked her features and figure, lingering in a manner that was positively insulting. Accustomed as she was to appreciative male attention, Chrissie felt her hackles rise as a new and strange sensation rippled through her body. Her heart began to thud, loudly and rhythmically, as if sounding a primeval warning of danger and, without conscious thought, she stiffened and straightened her shoulders, drawing herself up to her full height of five foot six inches as she turned to face him squarely.

'Miss Brennan?' he asked abruptly, his voice as deep and harsh as she'd have expected.

'Yes,' she nodded, nervously licking suddenly dry lips. Trent noticed the provocative gesture and his upper lip curled in disdain. Her tricks wouldn't work on him – he'd seen them all before.

'I'm Trent Fairfax,' he informed her coolly. And he's not just called in to say 'Hi' Chrissie thought uneasily. This was Torquemada, the Grand Inquisitor: she could understand why Ben had chosen the name. He was certainly stern and forbidding, although the full mouth was not that of an ascetic.

Does he think I've been leading Ben on? she wondered. Perhaps he was here to give her a lecture on her behaviour. According to Ben, the man bullied anyone and everyone with whom he came into contact.

'Yes?' she finally managed to respond, just as coolly – or so she hoped – feigning a calmness she was far from feeling.

'I want to speak to you – privately,' he added, with a pointed glance in Sally's direction, for the other girl was unashamedly watching and listening. Sally flushed when she caught his gaze and disappeared at speed: Chrissie wished fervently that she could follow her, but pride dictated that she stayed put.

'I'm sorry, I have work to do,' Chrissie said brusquely. If he had come to berate her for upsetting his little brother, he could just turn around and walk back out again, she fumed inwardly. Ben was twenty-four years old, even if only six or seven emotionally, and old enough to deal with life's disappointments without running to his big brother to sort out his problems for him.

Trent Fairfax took two long strides towards her and Chrissie had to force herself to stand her ground. She was suddenly glad she was wearing high heels.

'I'm not here to waste my time, Miss Brennan,' Trent said, calmly enough, but Chrissie's stomach lurched uncomfortably when she saw the menacing glitter in his eyes.

'What's going on out here?' Chrissie turned in relief as the manager hurried out of his office, alerted by Sally that something was amiss. Her relief was short-lived: unbeknown to her, Thomson and Wilson hoped to be sole selling agents for a new estate Fairfax Developments were building on the outskirts of Farminster.

'Ford, isn't it?' Trent extended his right hand, offering a brief handshake to the other man.

'Yes, yes it is,' Reg Ford smiled broadly. 'Good morning, Mr Fairfax. What can we do to be of help?' The man was positively gushing, Chrissie noted, her lip curling scornfully.

'I need to talk to Miss Brennan on a private matter. I'm sure you can spare her for an hour or so?' he asked, confident of not getting 'no' for an answer, Chrissie thought sourly. Perhaps he and Ben had more in common than she'd previously thought.

'Of course! No problem at all! Chrissie, take an early lunch hour,' he instructed.

'I'm not hungry yet,' she muttered defiantly, but a combined glare from both Trent Fairfax and Reg Ford made her go to fetch her bag and jacket from the cloakroom.

She deliberately lingered before going back out until it occurred to her that Trent Fairfax might be revelling in the belief that she was afraid to face him and she hurried back. Sally, still hovering but staying clear of the danger zone, raised a questioning brow as she emerged. Chrissie responded with a slight 'beats me' shrug of incomprehension.

'There's no need to hurry back; Sally can hold the fort for as long as necessary. It's good to see you again, Mr

Fairfax.' Reg Ford beamed once more and continued with his Uriah Heep impersonation as he practically bowed Trent Fairfax off the premises. God, what a creep he is, Chrissie thought disgustedly.

'Well?' she demanded mulishly, as soon as they were out on the pavement. 'What do you have to say that's so important?'

'Get into the car,' Trent jerked his head towards a silver-grey Mercedes parked illegally on double yellow lines.

'Why?' Chrissie didn't budge an inch: she had spotted a traffic warden bearing purposefully down on them and guessed from his demeanour that he wasn't made from the same boot-licking mould as Reg Ford. In fact, he gave the distinct impression of being highly delighted at the prospect of pasting a parking ticket on the windscreen of such a prestigious vehicle.

Trent had also noticed the guardian of the law approaching and, quick as a flash, opened the car door and bundled Chrissie inside before she realized his intention. He climbed in after her, his body hard against hers, and she had no choice but to scramble inelegantly across to the passenger seat. In the process, her skirt, short and slim-fitting, rode up around her thighs and she hastily tugged the hem down to her knees, uncomfortably aware of Trent's eyes lingering on the expanse of flesh before he gunned the engine into life and moved off, sketching a brief, mocking salute to the traffic warden as he drove past him.

'My brother's always had a liking for leggy blondes,' he remarked, matter-of-factly. In no way was it a compliment. 'But this is the first time he's offered marriage. You must be…' he paused, 'special.' The word was an insult, somehow suggesting she practised everything and anything listed in every sex manual ever written.

'Get to the point,' Chrissie snapped.

'Very well. Ben was in such a hurry to return here last night that he wrapped his car around a tree,' Trent told her bluntly, purposely omitting to mention that the site of the crash proved Ben had been on his way home, to the barn conversion in the grounds of Fairfax Hall.

Chrissie gave an involuntary cry of distress. Oh no! Had he been more upset than she had believed? He had certainly been angry enough to drive recklessly, even faster than he usually did – and that had been enough to frighten her witless on more than one occasion.

I shouldn't have quarrelled with him over the phone, she thought guiltily, knowing she had been so eager to extricate herself from an awkward situation that she had not stopped to consider possible consequences.

'Is he…badly hurt?' she whispered, her heart in her mouth as she waited for a reply.

'Bad enough to keep him in hospital for awhile: he has a broken leg, two broken ribs, concussion and an assortment of minor cuts and bruises,' Trent listed Ben's injuries and Chrissie winced.

'Not…nothing life-threatening?'

'Hopefully not, but he was unconscious for quite some time. No one knows how long he lay trapped in the wreckage until another driver spotted the car in the early hours and phoned for an ambulance. He's in St Anne's and, when he woke, he insisted on seeing you.' The icy glare which accompanied the last few words left Chrissie in no doubt that he considered her, at best, a nuisance, and that he wouldn't even give her the time of day if it weren't for Ben's request.

'So he has regained consciousness?' Chrissie realized,

greatly relieved that he wasn't in a coma or anything equally dreadful.

'More or less. He was drifting in and out of sleep when I left,' Trent said.

They lapsed into an uncomfortable silence. Chrissie sat back in the soft leather upholstery and tried to relax. Trent was a more careful and less impatient driver than Ben, she noted; he handled the large powerful car with competent speed as he drove to the hospital on the outskirts of town. His hands on the wheel and the controls were firm, yet relaxed…and on his finger he was wearing a wedding ring.

She had suddenly noticed the broad, plain gold ring, and the knowledge that he was married jolted her, although she couldn't have said why. But surely it was odd that Ben had never mentioned it? Yet perhaps not; after all, he had said little about his brother other than to complain that he was a tyrant, forever giving him grief for not pulling his weight in the family businesses.

She stole a look at Trent Fairfax's face and tried to recall what she knew about him, realizing that it was very little. She knew he was older than Ben by about ten years, which made him about thirty-three or thirty-four. She also knew that he had left university after their father's sudden death to take over the business, but nothing at all about his personal life, about a wife. Did he have children too? she wondered. Surely Ben would have mentioned the existence of nephews and nieces?

As if sensing her scrutiny, Trent turned suddenly to look at her sharply. Chrissie immediately averted her gaze, but couldn't resist watching him again when his attention returned to the road ahead.

In profile, he appeared even more stern, with dark

brows over a straight nose, the grooves around his mouth more noticeable. He most definitely did not have the look of a contented family man, she decided. The coldness and world-weary air had been part of his persona for some considerable time, she guessed, and had little to do with his present worry over Ben's accident or his anger with her… Exactly why is he angry with me? she frowned. The only reason, surely, was that Ben had told him they had quarrelled and now he was blaming her for the crash.

'I know about you and Charles Hawksworth,' Trent broke the silence suddenly. Chrissie blinked in surprise. What on earth had that got to do with anything?

'Excuse me?'

'You heard. You're not going to deny you're the girl the young fool was besotted with before his father packed him off to Australia out of harm's way?'

'How can I deny it when you put it so charmingly?' Chrissie retorted. 'Is it relevant?'

'I'm just giving you fair warning that I know about you. And I'll cut off Ben's money supply if he goes ahead with this ridiculous notion of marrying you.'

'If *he* goes ahead…?' Chrissie was stunned, and shook her head in disbelief. She fell silent, guessing there was no point in telling him she had rejected Ben's proposal. He wouldn't believe her, would think she was running scared. Still, as soon as Ben told this pig of a man that she had turned him down, well, he would just have to apologise! Relishing that prospect, she hunched her shoulders and let her mind drift back, almost five years, to the eventful time when she had met Charles…

She had still been at school, with nothing more to worry about than exams when her happy, uncomplicated childhood had come to an abrupt end. First, on a day she would never forget, her mother had been killed outright when a lorry driver lost control of his vehicle and ploughed into a group of pedestrians waiting at a bus stop in the town centre. The shock had caused her father to suffer a stroke, and a second attack, only days later, had proved fatal.

Neighbours and school teachers had rallied round, being wonderfully supportive, as had her friends' parents for a while, but then Social Services had stepped in and taken over.

Chrissie had hated the children's home, and spent as little time there as possible. But she had seen little of her schoolfriends; it hadn't seemed right, going out to clubs or the cinema, or hanging about the shopping arcade on a Saturday as she used to. Instead she had cycled around the countryside alone, re-visiting childhood haunts, prefer-ring her own company as she struggled to come to terms with what had happened to her.

It was while on one of her cycle rides that she had encountered Charles Hawksworth. He had been out riding his horse and had spotted the golden-haired long-legged girl eating her picnic lunch on the bank of the river that flowed through his father's fields. He had reined in his horse and called out to her.

'Hey! You're trespassing, you know. There's a penalty for that – either you go to prison or you give me a kiss!' He had spoken in jest, of course, and had been appalled when Chrissie burst into tears, believing himself respon-sible for her distress.

Jumping quickly from the saddle and tethering the horse to a conveniently low branch, he had knelt down beside her.

'I was only joking, you know. You're not doing any harm here,' he had begun awkwardly, laying a tentative hand on her shoulder.

'I know; I'm not crying because of you,' Chrissie had sniffed, raising tear-drenched eyes to his and trying to smile. He had taken one look into her large, blue-violet eyes and been instantly smitten. And, when he knew her story, he was determined to look after her.

Chrissie, vulnerable and lonely, revelled in his 'love' for her, desperately needing someone to try and replace some of what she had lost. Later, they both realized it had been puppy love, if that, perhaps merely infatuation. Charles, only eighteen, fuelled by a potent mixture of chivalry and lust, had wanted to marry her, and Chrissie thought she wanted that, too, when what she had really wanted was to belong, to be part of a family again.

Charles's father, James Hawksworth had intervened at that point, kindly but firmly saying that they were too young to consider marriage. It had already been arranged that Charles was to spend some years with an uncle in Australia and James insisted he went as planned. If Charles and Chrissie still felt the same way about each other after a year's separation, he promised, he would allow them to marry.

Of course, as James Hawksworth had known, a year later their feelings had changed; they had both moved on. They were still in contact, but ever more rarely and now, after nearly five years, Charles was still living happily in Australia and he and Chrissie exchanged Christmas cards, nothing more. Charles Hawksworth was only a fond memory as far as Chrissie was concerned – and she was sure that he felt the same way about her.

'What are you plotting, I wonder?' Trent broke

suddenly into her reverie. Chrissie blinked, brought abruptly back to the present by his hateful, sneering voice.

'I was wondering who to get my claws into now that you've rumbled me!' she retorted.

'I wouldn't be a bit surprised,' Trent muttered. 'Don't look in my direction.'

'I'm not that desperate!' she shot back. Trent's mouth tightened, but he said nothing more, for they had arrived at the hospital.

As he swung into the car park, Chrissie stared up at its edifice and felt her flash crawl. The ambulance had brought her mother's body here, and later her father had lain here, unmoving, until he died. She didn't want to go inside and was almost grateful when Trent put a restraining hand on her arm as she fumbled for the door handle.

'Before we go inside, there's the small matter of the ring to settle,' he said evenly.

'The ring?'

'Don't play dumb! Ben told me he gave it to you. Well, he had no right to do that, engagement or no engagement. It's a valuable family heirloom and the bank had no authority to release it without my signature. As soon as they realized their error, they contacted me, which is why I sent for the young fool yesterday. So, don't mess me about, Miss Brennan,' he bit out, obviously holding on to his temper with great difficulty. 'That ring is, strictly speaking, stolen property and I want it back.'

'I...I don't have it,' she stammered.

'Of course you do. Unless you've pawned it already?' he asked, his voice dangerously quiet.

'Of course not! I told you, I don't have it. Ben does.'

'That had better be true, young lady.'

Chrissie felt herself flush with indignation. 'Of course it's bloody true!' she snapped, furious with herself for feeling intimidated by him. 'What would I possibly have to gain by lying? Oh, this is too ridiculous for words,' she went on, reaching again for the door handle. 'Let's go and ask Ben. Presumably you'll believe *him*?'

chapter three

Chrissie stalked off towards the entrance, hoping her legs didn't look as wobbly as they felt. She'd hate for him to guess how much she was shaking.

Trent caught up with her easily and pushed open the door, automatically allowing her to precede him, she noted. Or perhaps he was afraid she'd run away if he wasn't guarding her retreat.

'One more thing…' he began.

'Oh God!' Chrissie raised her eyes heavenwards.

'My mother's here,' Trent continued, ignoring her interruption. 'Naturally she's already distressed by what's happened to Ben and I don't want her further upset by any arguments over the ring.'

'Very well,' Chrissie shrugged. As far as she was concerned there need be no argument. One simple question to Ben would clear the whole thing up. 'On condition you apologise when you're proved wrong,' she added sweetly. Trent didn't answer, but merely motioned for her to go inside.

Chrissie hadn't set foot in St Anne's since her father's death and memories flooded back as the over-warm, antiseptic smell of the hospital assailed her nostrils and caught at the back of her throat.

Trent didn't notice her instinctive recoil and, disdaining use of the lift, began climbing the flight of stairs, taking them two at a time. Since Chrissie had no idea where Ben was to be found, she had no option but to follow him, stumbling a little, hampered by a short skirt and high heels, and hating Trent Fairfax more with every step she took.

Fortunately for her, Trent veered off at the top of the first flight and strode along the corridor which led to the private wing. The floor was highly polished – did these people hope to drum up business by causing more broken limbs to visitors? she found herself wondering, as she almost cannoned into him when he came to an abrupt stop.

'Wait here a moment,' he instructed, then quietly opened the door. 'Mother?' he called softly. 'I'm back.'

'Oh, thank God.' Celia Fairfax hurried from the room and Chrissie braced herself for more hostility. But Celia smiled at her, albeit rather absently, before turning to her older son. 'The police have been here – I told them to wait and talk to you but they insisted on speaking to Ben alone. He hadn't been drinking, had he?'

'Even Ben's not that stupid,' Trent said, with what Chrissie supposed was his idea of reassurance. 'Don't worry; I'll have a word with them. I might need to discuss another matter with them,' he added, with a meaningful glance at Chrissie.

She ignored him, with what she hoped was a haughty expression, and instead studied Ben's mother. Obviously she was anxious and flustered now, but Chrissie guessed she was normally a very well-groomed lady. She must be in her fifties, but didn't look it; she was slim, her body toned, her hair still a pale blonde that didn't appear to be helped along by the hairdresser, and cut into a well-shaped bob that framed a sweet face.

She was wearing a chic suit and had even remembered to don her pearls. She was perfectly groomed – except that the buttons on her jacket were fastened incorrectly, giving it a lopsided appearance which, Chrissie guessed, was quite out of character, and due only to her present anxiety.

Trent noticed the buttons, too, and silently reached out and re-fastened them, evidently knowing his mother would hate to be seen dressed less than immaculately. Chrissie found his action oddly touching, as if he were the parent and Celia the child.

'Ma, this is Chrissie Brennan.'

'Hello, dear,' Celia smiled.

'How do you do?' Chrissie returned the smile, a little shyly, still rather wary after Trent's hostility. 'How's Ben?'

'The doctor says he'll be fine, but it will be quite some time before he's up and about. I was so worried when I saw him earlier,' her lower lip trembled slightly, 'but he seems much better already, far more lucid.'

'That'll make a nice change,' Trent muttered.

'You're too hard on him,' Mrs Fairfax responded, rather automatically, Chrissie thought, as if she had said the same thing many times before.

'We haven't met before, have we, dear?' Celia turned to Chrissie, but didn't wait for an answer – a trait that those who knew her quickly became familiar with – and turned to Trent.

'I'm delighted you've brought her, but it's such a pity it has to be under these circumstances. Are you staying for the weekend, Chrissie?' she rattled on. Chrissie frowned in perplexity but had no chance to say anything.

'Please do stay,' Celia urged. 'I can easily have a spare room prepared – or are you happy to share with Trent? Oh, I know how things are these days,' she went on indulgently, completely oblivious to Chrissie's glazed expression and Trent's increasingly exasperated attempts to stem the flow.

'I don't mind a bit; I'm very broadminded – I have to be, with two sons – but, after Francesca, I was beginning to wonder if Trent would ever settle down again. I know there have been other women over the years, of course, but you're the only one he's brought home to meet me, so…'

'Mother!' Trent yelled, his voice seeming louder than it really was in the hushed atmosphere of the hospital.

'Yes, dear?' Celia finally paused for breath.

'Chrissie is NOT with me. She's a friend of Ben's and he insisted on seeing her. You know perfectly well that I arrived home alone this morning,' he added, more gently.

'Yes, well, Chrissie could have followed you by train…' Celia was reluctant to give up on her idea.

'But she didn't. She lives here in Farminster. Why don't you go and have a coffee, or wait in my car while she speaks with Ben for a few minutes? I don't think he should have too many visitors at one time,' he added, glibly explaining away his desire to have his mother out of the way while he cleared up the matter of the emerald.

'I think I will have a coffee; it's so stuffy in here. Don't stay long, though; he's supposed to get as much rest as possible.'

'We won't. We'll meet you downstairs shortly,' he assured her. 'Inside,' he instructed Chrissie tersely, as soon as Celia was out of earshot.

Chrissie took a deep breath and steeled herself to enter the room, still a little fearful of what she might find despite Celia's assurances that he was going to get well.

But Ben was awake and smiled when he saw her. He was deathly pale, apart from an obscenely-red stitched cut on his right temple, and lay flat on his back, his right leg heavily encased in plaster and supported by an array of pulleys.

As Chrissie walked over to the bed, she saw that his ribs were bandaged and there was dark bruising on his right arm and shoulder.

'Plastered again, Ben?' she couldn't resist saying, pointing to the cast on his leg. Ben grinned.

'You sound like the cops. They've taken the car, Trent,' he looked beyond her to his brother, who was leaning back against the door, arms folded across his chest as he watched Chrissie closely. 'They're going to check for mechanical failure, but I got the impression they think I was speeding.'

'Were you?' Trent asked.

'Can't remember, could have been,' he admitted, unabashed.

'Ben, you weren't upset about the phone call, were you?' Chrissie asked, perching gingerly on the edge of the bed.

'Finally got you into bed!' Ben winked. 'What phone call?'

'You phoned me from a call box when you were on your way back from London,' she reminded him.

'A call box?' he frowned. 'Sorry, can't remember.'

'What *do* you remember?' Trent asked, while it was slowly dawning on Chrissie that Ben had forgotten that she had rejected his proposal. Oh no! She'd have to do it again!

'I certainly remember being lectured by you,' Ben grumbled, 'and I had a kip at your place before I came home. But I can't really remember the drive; I seem to recall the traffic in London was awful,' his brow creased and he winced. 'I've got a filthy headache.'

'OK, don't worry about that now,' Trent said quickly. 'You need to sleep. But first, I do need to find that ring.'

'The emerald? What about it?'

'He thinks I stole it,' Chrissie put in bitterly.

'Course she didn't!' Ben glared at Trent and Chrissie turned and shot him a look of triumph.

'Tell him where it is, Ben,' she said confidently.

'I don't know – I gave it to you,' he looked puzzled. Chrissie's smile faded a little.

'Ben, I gave it back. I put it in your jacket pocket,' she said, rather feverishly. She knew Trent was watching her intently, a slight frown darkening his features. 'The tan leather one,' she added.

'You were still wearing that when you came to my office,' Trent put in.

'Yeah, I don't think I ever got to bed on Wednesday night – I was crashed out on the sofa when you rang…' he rubbed his aching head. Chrissie bit her lip: it was obvious he needed to rest, but she was beginning to panic now, desperate to locate the wretched ring.

'So you must have had the jacket with you when you had the accident. Is the jacket here in the hospital? Or still in the car?'

'I'll check with the staff here, and then the police, if necessary. Come on, Miss Brennan; Ben must get some sleep now,' Trent said firmly. Chrissie hesitated, then nodded and got to her feet. Hopefully Ben would remember, when his mind and body had begun to recover from the trauma of the crash.

'Come again soon, won't you?' Ben caught at her hand, his eyes pleading.

'Of course I will,' she bent and kissed his uninjured cheek.

'My mother will be waiting,' Trent said curtly, opening the door. Chrissie straightened and walked towards him. 'I'll drive you back to your office.'

'That's not necessary, I can catch the bus. Although, if you hadn't practically kidnapped me earlier, I could have come here in my own car,' she snapped.

'I said, I'll drive you,' he repeated and put a hand on her arm as she was about to flounce off. Chrissie halted unwillingly and glanced pointedly at his restraining hand. Once again, she noted the gleam of his wedding ring and recalled his mother's mention of Francesca. Presumably she was his wife, but separated or divorced since Celia hoped he would find someone else. Fat chance until he lightened up, she thought. Perhaps he didn't want to; as he still wore the ring, it was logical to assume his wife had left him, not the reverse. Which went some way towards explaining his bad temper and rudeness, but certainly didn't excuse it, she decided, thrusting down an unwarranted feeling of compassion for the cold, proud man standing beside her.

'Do you mind?' she asked frostily, for he continued to hold her arm in a vice-like grip. He frowned and looked down at his hand, almost as if he was unaware of what he had been doing, then released her with impolite haste.

'What did you mean when you asked Ben if he'd been upset by your phone call?' he demanded, as they walked down the stairs. 'What did you say to him?'

Chrissie hesitated: much as she would like to get Trent Fairfax off her back, she had a feeling that he wouldn't believe her if she told the truth: that she'd rejected Ben's proposal. He would probably think she was scared of him.

'That's between Ben and me,' she said bravely. 'It's none of your business.'

'Perhaps not. But the whereabouts of that ring most certainly is my business,' he warned her. 'I intend to find it.'

'The sooner, the better,' she told him. 'I've told you the truth – I put it back inside the breast pocket of Ben's tan leather jacket.'

'Why?'

'Why…what?' she was taken aback by the question barked at her.

'Why did you give it back?' *If* you did, his tone implied. 'Why didn't you hang on to it, flaunt it, show it off to your friends – isn't that what girls usually do with engagement rings?' Again, Chrissie hesitated, but she was convinced he would only believe the truth when he heard it from Ben.

'It was too big. Now, can I get back to work?

They locked glances for a moment, then Trent nodded. 'Very well.'

Celia Fairfax was already sitting in the front passenger seat and smiled at Chrissie with seemingly genuine warmth. Chrissie slid into the rear seat when Trent silently opened the door for her, returned Celia's smile and relaxed a little; after all, Trent had made it clear he didn't want any unpleasantness in front of his mother, so she figured she would be safe on the trip back to town.

Celia half-turned in her seat so that she could talk to both Chrissie and Trent, and her eyes, almost as vivid a blue as those of her older son, were alight with kindly curiosity as she bombarded Chrissie with questions about her job.

'You can drop me in Market Street, too,' she said to Trent. 'I must buy Ben some pyjamas – I looked for some this morning, but he doesn't seem to own any,' she explained.

'Fine, but stay away from the auction rooms,' Trent told her.

'Ooh, is there an auction today? Just what I need to take my mind off things! I…'

'No,' Trent said firmly.

'Honestly! One tiny mistake…'

'Tiny! You came home with a massive, hideous desk that you hadn't even bid for,' he sighed.

'How on earth did you manage to do that?' Chrissie had to ask.

'Well, I was waving to Mrs Featherby across the room. She's as blind as a bat nowadays, poor thing, and didn't see me…anyway, the auctioneer thought I was bidding and it was such a nice desk I decided to keep it…'

'It was riddled with woodworm!' Trent cut her off. 'Half the panelling in the library was infested before I noticed and chucked it out.'

'Yes, well, that was unfortunate,' Celia agreed. 'But it wasn't hideous; I liked it,' she insisted, then turned back to Chrissie. 'The auctioneer told me it had five secret compartments,' she confided. 'I found three. Such fun,' she beamed, then switched her attention back to Trent. 'As you'll be here this weekend, do you think you could look at my bank statements? And perhaps give me a cheque? I'm sure they've made a mistake; I can't possibly have spent that much money.'

Chrissie made no attempt to hide her grin when Trent took one hand off the wheel and raked it through his hair, exasperation evident in every movement. For a moment, he caught her eye in the rear-view mirror, and there was no hostility in his gaze, just a rueful acceptance of her amusement.

'I'll take a look,' he agreed, and Chrissie knew from his tone that he didn't expect to find any banking errors, only extravagant spending.

She found herself feeling almost sorry for him – why hadn't Celia asked Ben for help? On second thoughts, perhaps that wouldn't be a good idea. Ben claimed never to open his bank statements and would no doubt advise his mother to do likewise. But it seemed that Celia and Ben, both adults, relied on Trent for everything. Then she remembered how much he enjoyed the financial power he held over his family, and the brief feeling of empathy vanished.

Trent drew to a halt outside the estate agency and Chrissie scrambled out of the car.

'I'm so pleased to have met you,' she said to Celia, pointedly ignoring Trent. He smiled slightly at her emphasis on the 'you'.

'Same here, dear. I do hope we'll meet again soon,' Celia smiled.

'I'll be in touch about that other matter,' Trent said.

'Good. I'll look forward to hearing your apology,' Chrissie retorted, with a confidence that surprised him. He watched thoughtfully as she walked into the office, then put the Mercedes into gear and moved off. He'd drop his mother at the arcade, well away from the auction rooms on Market Street, and then go in search of that wretched ring. He found himself hoping he would find it amongst Ben's possessions.

'Well? How is he? Reg said Mr Fairfax told him Ben was in a car crash.' Sally was agog for news. 'Why is he so angry with you? If looks could kill…' she shivered.

'Ben's a bit battered and bruised, but he's going to be all right,' Chrissie said, answering the first question and ignoring the second. 'Why don't you go for lunch now I'm back?'

'OK. Have you eaten?'

'No, I'm not hungry,' Chrissie shook her head. Her stomach was churning, though she wasn't sure whether that was caused by the sight of Ben's injuries or by Trent's verbal assault.

'I'll bring you a sandwich, shall I?' Sally asked.

'Thanks,' Chrissie didn't think she would be able to eat it, but appreciated the offer.

She was kept quite busy during Sally's absence, with a constant stream of would-be buyers and sellers, both calling into the office and on the telephone. She was glad to be occupied, but pleased there was nothing to tax her brain too much. She didn't feel at all capable of dealing with any complications regarding mortgages or solicitors.

'Here you are,' Sally dropped a packet of ham sandwiches on to Chrissie's desk, plus an early edition of the *Farminster Echo*. 'There's a small piece about Ben's crash.'

'Oh, thanks.' Chrissie unfolded the paper and read the article, wincing as the Porsche was described as a 'write-off' and Ben as 'lucky to be alive'. Then, 'The rotten bastard!' she exclaimed.

'Who?' Sally asked.

'Trent bloody Fairfax!' Chrissie fumed. 'I've been feeling really guilty about the crash because he led me to believe that Ben was on his way to see me when it happened. But he wasn't; according to this, he was on the other side of town, not far from Fairfax Hall!'

'Mmm, that's interesting. Didn't you say he had summoned Ben to London? So, in a way, it's *his* fault,' Sally pointed out. 'Perhaps he's feeling guilty, too – it's always comforting to be able to lay the blame on someone else's shoulders, isn't it?'

'You could be right,' Chrissie nodded. 'Sally, do you…?' she began to ask if she knew of Trent's marriage, but was prevented by the ringing of her phone. When she had dealt with that query, Sally was busy with another, and so it continued for the rest of the afternoon.

There was no chance for a lengthy chat until almost five, when most people were heading home for the weekend. Then they finally sat down over a cup of tea while sending out sales brochures which had been requested by phone.

'I was going to ask you earlier about Trent Fairfax – did you know that he's been married? She was called Francesca, I think.'

Sally frowned in concentration. 'How long ago?'

'I've no idea. Quite a while ago, probably.' Chrissie remembered what Celia had said about other women and her desire for him to settle down again. 'It's odd, because Ben's never mentioned having a sister-in-law.'

'He'd have no reason to, if they divorced,' Sally said. 'Actually, I don't know much at all about Trent Fairfax. He's quite a bit older than us, isn't he? We could have been at primary school when he got married!'

'Yes,' Chrissie agreed, rather doubtfully. 'But it would have been the wedding of the year, wouldn't it? Surely we'd remember.'

'Not necessarily. It's the bride's family who arranges the wedding, isn't it? Unless she was local, there probably wouldn't have been more than a couple of photos in the paper,' she pointed out.

'Of course,' Chrissie nodded her agreement.

'Why are you so interested?

'I'm not sure,' she replied truthfully. 'He seems so unhappy.'

'He just seemed angry to me – I was glad it was you he was looking for and not me!' Sally said feelingly. 'Even if Ben *had* been driving recklessly because he wanted to see you, Trent can hardly hold you responsible – he must know Ben's always speeding. Everyone else around here does!'

'Yes, but that's not the only reason for his anger,' Chrissie said slowly, needing to unburden herself. 'You know I told you about Ben's so-called proposal on Wednesday night?'

'Sure.'

'Did I mention an emerald ring?'

'No! he gave you a ring? Let's have a look,' she asked eagerly. Chrissie sighed.

'I can't; I gave it back. But the trouble is, Sally,' Chrissie's voice rose in her agitation. Reg Ford, in his office behind them with the door ajar, raised his head and listened intently. 'The bloody thing's gone missing! And Trent Fairfax thinks I stole it. Apparently it's a valuable family heirloom and should never have been taken out of the bank.'

'Oh God,' Sally stared at her.

'What am I going to do?' Chrissie asked. 'He even threatened to report it to the police.'

'He won't do that,' Sally tried to comfort her. 'He can't, not if Ben gave it to you. That can't be called stealing.'

'That's what Trent Fairfax calls it,' Chrissie sniffed, near to tears. She felt very frightened, very alone and absolutely exhausted.

'Forget him, for a few hours at least. You didn't eat that sandwich at lunchtime, so you must eat this evening,' Sally said firmly. 'You're going to go home, have a long hot bath and then come out with me for a meal and a glass or two of wine to relax you.'

'That's very kind of you, Sally, but I'm too tired…'

'No, you're not, you're depressed,' Sally contradicted her. 'You'll only brood if you stay at home.'

'I ought to go to the hospital,' Chrissie demurred.

'Not tonight; you might bump into Trent Fairfax again. You can visit Ben tomorrow. Tonight, you're going to unwind. I insist. And I'll drive, so you can drown your sorrows.'

'OK, thanks.' Chrissie managed a wan smile.

Reg Ford bustled out of his office at that moment, checking his watch.

'Time to go home, ladies,' he said genially. 'I'll finish up here.' They didn't need telling twice.

'Thanks. Goodnight.'

'Goodnight.' He locked the door behind them, then turned and bounded up the stairs to where the owner, Dan Thomson, was sitting in his luxurious office.

'Excuse me, sir,' Reg rapped lightly on the open door. 'I've just heard something interesting which could help us clinch the deal with Fairfax. I think he would be happier awarding us the contract if we got rid of Miss Brennan.'

Chrissie felt much better after soaking in a hot bath and began to look forward to an evening out with Sally. She phoned the hospital and was told Ben was sleeping, so her guilt over not visiting him abated.

Her spirits rose as she put on make-up and dressed, choosing a scarlet lace mini dress and matching red high-heeled shoes. Perhaps it was a bit over the top for an inexpensive meal with a girlfriend, but it made her feel good. She was beginning to feel very hungry, so when Sally knocked on the door ten minutes early, she hurried to open it.

'I'm glad you're… Oh!' It was Trent Fairfax. He looked her up and down, very slowly, from the tips of her stiletto-heeled shoes to the top of her gleaming, newly-washed hair.

'Hospital visiting?' he drawled.

'No,' Chrissie flushed. 'I phoned earlier. He's asleep.' She knew she sounded defensive.

'So you feel free to…?' one dark brow was raised in enquiry.

'Go out with a friend. A girlfriend,' she clarified. 'Sally Farmer, from the office…oh, it's none of your business!' she snapped, furious with herself for explaining her actions, as well as with him for his implied criticism.

'What are you doing here? And how did you find me?' He arched his brow even further and there was a glint of sardonic amusement in the blue eyes.

'Telephone directory,' he said dryly.

'Oh.' Chrissie felt a fool for asking, but recovered quickly. 'What do you want? My friend will be here soon.'

'And we don't want to keep him waiting, do we?'

'Her,' Chrissie corrected. Trent decided to stop baiting her.

'May I come in?' He jerked his head slightly to where Chrissie's next-door neighbour was hovering in her garden, agog with curiosity.

'Very well. I'd offer you a drink but I've run out of arsenic.' She pulled open the door and stepped back, allowing him to enter, stiffening a little as he glanced quickly, dismissively around her cottage. It didn't take long; downstairs was comprised of hall, open plan sitting room with a tiny dining area and the kitchen beyond.

Chrissie braced herself for a disparaging comment – she supposed he wasn't accustomed to visiting people who lived in two-up, two-down terraced cottages. Since he had inherited a mansion, he probably looked down on ordinary working people who needed to earn money to buy or rent modest housing. She was too flustered by him to remember, or care, that Trent had worked hard to build up the family business and that, of the two brothers, it was Ben who was the idle playboy.

'It's lucky you don't suffer from hay fever,' was what he actually said, noting the profusion of red roses, in vases and jugs, placed on every available surface. 'Ben?'

'Yes.'

'Original,' his lip curled slightly. Chrissie, forgetting she'd thought the same, immediately bristled at his tone.

'What would you choose?'

'For you? A one-way plane ticket to anywhere you want,' he shot back.

'How about Australia?' Chrissie asked sweetly, trying to hide the hurt she felt at his relentless hostility, and recalling his attack on her regarding Charles Hawksworth. 'I could go and visit Charles.'

'No chance. The Hawksworth's have never done me any harm. Now, about the ring,' he said briskly, 'Ben's jacket was in the car – the police are still checking it over, but so far they've found his wallet and his mobile phone, but no ring.'

'It must be there!' Chrissie said desperately. Trent regarded her thoughtfully for a moment.

'It's possible Ben took it to a jeweller to have it altered before he left London yesterday,' he said, wondering why he was playing Devil's Advocate. It was just that she looked so…stricken.

'So you do believe me?' Chrissie asked. He hesitated.

'Let's just say that the ring is currently lost property,'

he said, and she nodded. That was a distinct improvement on "stolen property", which was how he'd described it earlier. She could only hope Ben's memory would return, and the sooner, the better. She offered Trent a tentative smile and, with more of an effort than he cared to acknowledge, he hardened his heart, and his voice.

'Where are you really going tonight?' he demanded harshly.

Chrissie decided that she'd had enough. Ben was prone to jealous outbursts and, with any luck, Trent would repeat what she was about to say and Ben would dump her. End of 'engagement'. Brilliant!

'OK, I'll tell you,' she feigned capitulation. 'I'm going to the Forester's Arms,' she said, hoping he knew it was the most disreputable pub in town, notorious for fights and drugs, and where no 'nice' girl would be seen dead. He knew.

'Really?' He didn't bat an eyelid. 'That's hardly suitable for a girl like you,' he remarked, much to Chrissie's surprise. And to her pleasure, she discovered.

'Why not?' she asked breathlessly.

'The…er…patrons of that establishment aren't wealthy enough to interest you,' he said snidely. The crushing disappointment nearly reduced her to tears. Then she felt an almost overwhelming urge to attack him, with her fists, nails, feet – anything, in fact, that might make an impression on him and preferably scar him for life. Just in time, she remembered her reason for mentioning the wretched pub and forced herself to speak calmly.

'Money isn't everything,' she shrugged. 'Manual workers have a certain…earthy charm, a machismo that rich men so often lack,' she explained sweetly, enjoying the expression of incredulous anger on his haughty face.

'I find that too much soft living tends to emasculate a man…' She broke off abruptly when he made an instinctive move towards her, exultant that she had pierced his cool façade, but then he checked and smiled at her, albeit rather wolfishly she thought in sudden trepidation.

'Are you by any chance challenging me to prove my masculinity?' he asked, the intense blue of his eyes holding her in thrall.

'I…er…yes!' She was startled to hear herself saying. Trent blinked, as if she had surprised him, too, then he bent his head towards her.

Chrissie closed her eyes as the tantalising, male scent of him filled her nostrils and her lips parted in eager anticipation.

'You little slut,' he said softly, his breath warm on her cheek. Chrissie's eyes shot open and she felt as if she had been doused in ice-cold water.

'I…I was just…' she began desperately, but with no idea how to explain the inexplicable.

'I know what you were doing – and I'm not interested,' he said coolly, and hoped she didn't guess he was lying. He needn't have worried; there was nothing in his gaze to suggest anything other than boredom and distaste.

Chrissie felt more humiliated than she had ever done in her life and knew her cheeks must be as red as her dress. She dropped her gaze, unable to face his contempt and heard, rather than saw, him move to the door and wrench it open. After it banged shut behind him, she sank to the floor and held her head in her hands. What on earth had possessed her?

chapter four

'I don't understand,' Sally said, for the umpteenth time. 'Why on earth did you say you were going to the Forester's Arms?'

'I don't know!' Chrissie wailed, refilling her glass. She had already drunk three large glasses of wine while they were waiting for their main meal to be served, yet she was still shaking from her encounter with Trent Fairfax. 'He refused to believe me when I said I was coming out with you… oh, I dunno, maybe I thought he'd pass it on to Ben and then Ben would dump me…'

'Have you lost your mind?' Sally stared at her. 'If Ben gets mad at you, he'll probably want that ring back, too!'

'Oh God!' Chrissie buried her head in her hands: that thought had never occurred to her.

'Seriously, Chrissie, you need Ben on your side,' Sally warned, then they both fell silent while the waiter placed the food in front of them. 'What are you going to do if the ring isn't found?'

'Go to prison, probably,' she said dolefully, ignoring her food but topping up her glass again.

'That's silly, and you know it. The ring is just lost some-where, but, until it's found you'd be daft to alienate Ben. Now, eat your food.'

'He called me a slut.'

'Ben did?' Sally paused, fork midway to her mouth.

'No, Trent.' Chrissie squished bits of her pizza together, oozing melted cheese out on to her plate.

'Well, it's hardly surprising if he thinks you're a regular at the Forester's Arms,' Sally pointed out.

'That's not when he said it,' Chrissie muttered, and emptied her glass again. The memory would *not* go away. Right now she envied Ben his amnesia more than anything. Crashing her car to obtain it did seem rather drastic, but she found herself considering it.

'When, then?'

'Well…' Chrissie blushed anew. 'I made a terrible mistake. You see, I thought he was going to kiss me,' she mumbled.

'Kiss you? From what I saw of Trent Fairfax this morning, he's more likely to throttle you!'

'I know!' Chrissie pushed her plate aside and reached for the almost empty wine bottle. 'That's what's so idiotic! He's made it perfectly plain he thinks I'm a gold-digging thief and, yet, I really thought he was going to kiss me! There's no excuse for such stupidity,' she shook her head mournfully and found she couldn't stop talking. 'Perhaps I should stick with Ben after all – we're both immature and stupid. At least he can blame alcohol for his behaviour – but I don't drink.'

'You're doing a good impersonation tonight,' Sally said tartly. She wrested the bottle from Chrissie's hand and signalled to the waiter, asking him to bring strong black coffee.

'Let's swap shifts this weekend,' Sally suggested next. The agency hired extra staff for Saturdays and Sundays, with the experienced Chrissie and Sally working one day each. 'I'll cover for you tomorrow and you can work on Sunday. Reg Ford won't mind, so long as one of us turns up. Spend the day trying to sort this mess out.'

'How?' Chrissie sighed.

'For starters, go and see Ben, just in case Trent does decide to tell him you've been to the Forester's Arms; think hard about where the ring could be and, most important of all, try and make peace with Trent Fairfax!'

It was good advice, but hard to follow, Chrissie thought next morning when she was trying to shake off her headache and lethargy under a cool shower.

Except for the visiting Ben bit, and even that could be tricky. If he had regained his memory, he might be mad at her and demand she return his ring, and if he hadn't remembered and she went along with his delusion that they were engaged, she would only further enrage Trent. Oh God, Trent…please don't let me bump into him today, she prayed. Better still, let him have developed amnesia, too.

When she phoned the hospital, she was transferred to Ben's room. He sounded almost his old self, but was already bored by his confinement.

'Are you coming to see me?' he asked plaintively.

'Of course I am. But you won't want everyone coming at the same time,' she said, pleased by her quick thinking. 'When will your family be there?' she asked, trying to sound ultra casual.

'I spoke to Mum earlier – Trent's bringing her over this afternoon.'

'Great! Er, so it will be better if I come this evening, won't it? About seven?'

'Not until then? Oh, I suppose you're working…'

'See you later,' Chrissie interrupted and replaced the receiver, giving vent to a huge sigh of relief. A reprieve. She now knew how to avoid Trent Fairfax for today, and presumably he'd be returning to London tomorrow?

Surely the blasted ring would have turned up before his next trip to Farminster?

Annabel was Ben's first visitor of the day, typically arriving before visiting hours and treating with contempt the nurse who tried to tell her to return later.

'I can't, I'm off to London for the weekend,' she said, as if that settled it. 'Room 26, isn't it? I won't stay long, I can't abide hospitals.'

'Hello, darling,' she burst into Ben's room without knocking. 'Thought you'd need cheering up since you're missing Sophie's bash.' She stooped and kissed his cheek, handed him a 'get well' card and brandished a bottle of orange juice. 'Bucks Fizz, darling. A waste of champers, if you ask me, but I thought it might be confiscated if I didn't disguise it!'

'Thanks,' Ben brightened. 'Just what I needed,' he said, gulping from the glass she filled for him. He eyed her slender form in its white mini-dress as she draped herself over the foot of his bed. She had a triangular mole on the top of her thigh and the sight triggered a hazy memory. He struggled to remember.

'Wednesday night,' he frowned. 'Did we…?'

'No, you were legless, darling,' Annabel shook her head regretfully. 'We had fun, though, but nothing for what's-her-name to worry about. It was her fault, anyway, for disappearing and leaving you alone. Where is she – Christy, is it?'

'Chrissie,' Ben corrected, grinning. As Annabel knew damn well!

'Whatever,' Annabel shrugged dismissively. 'Why isn't she here, mopping your fevered brow?' she asked, rather waspishly.

'She's working.'

'It beats me why women make such a fuss about having jobs,' she sniffed. 'It seems very dreary to me.'

'And me. They have bills to pay,' Ben told her airily. She was a royal bitch, but she amused him.

'Why don't they just ask their parents for money?' Annabel was genuinely perplexed.

'Or an older brother!' Ben held out his glass for a refill. 'Let's have some more booze and make a toast – to those who pay the bills and leave the rest of us free to enjoy ourselves!'

Annabel touched her glass to his, then surveyed him steadily, serious now.

'Are you free, Ben? You're not really going to marry that girl, are you? I couldn't believe it when you proposed! And neither could she, judging by the look on her face,' she added. 'She didn't seem to be exactly thrilled.'

'She was just surprised,' Ben mumbled. His memory of the events of the past few days was still shrouded in fog, but occasionally the grey mist lifted and he now had the impression that Chrissie had turned him down. Perhaps some low-life sneak had told her he had left the party with Annabel? If so, he was pretty sure he could talk her round.

'We were all surprised, darling,' Annabel eyed him thoughtfully for a moment, then lost interest. For now. She was confident she could take Ben away from Chrissie any time she wanted to, but as he obviously was going to be no fun at all for quite some time, she would wait until he was back on his feet before making a move.

'Must go,' she reached over and kissed his mouth. 'I'll pop in next week and fill you in on all the gossip.' She stood up and sashayed over to the door, then paused. 'By the way, darling, in case you haven't noticed, I've got green eyes. That emerald would look much better on me,' she drawled.

Chrissie drove slowly into the hospital grounds, cautiously scanning the rows of parked cars for a glimpse of Trent's Mercedes, ready to execute a nifty three-point turn and head for home if he were still here. However, there was no sign of it, so she parked and went inside.

'Hi,' she smiled warmly at Ben, and placed the magazines and card she had brought on his bedside locker. 'How are you feeling?'

'Awful,' he muttered. The Bucks Fizz had not mixed well with his medication. He was also in pain and felt both bored and depressed.

'I'm sorry to hear that,' Chrissie regarded him sympathetically.

'You're late,' he grumbled.

'No, I'm not. I said I'd be here at seven,' she reminded him, but received no reply.

'I see you've got loads of cards already,' she went on brightly. One of the nurses had set them out on the window sill. Still no response.

'May I look at them?' she asked. What she really wanted to ask was whether he had yet remembered what he had done with the ring, but she sensed that he would say 'no' out of sheer perversity. He was wearing the sulky schoolboy expression she was used to seeing when he didn't get his own way.

'I met your mother yesterday,' she said next, having read the cards and pulled up a chair beside the bed. 'I thought she was really nice and very attractive. She doesn't look her age, does she?'

'She certainly doesn't act it,' he growled. 'She drives Trent and me mad.'

'I should imagine most people drive Trent mad,' Chrissie responded tartly; then, ultra casually, 'You never told me he'd been married?'

'More than my life's worth!' Ben told her. 'Anyway, it was years ago; about time he got over it,' he said callously, then he smiled for the first time. 'Talking of Trent – you'll never guess what's happened!'

'What?' Chrissie eyed him uncertainly; there was nothing nice about his smile.

'He's got a black eye!' Ben told her, not bothering to hide his glee. 'Someone tried to nick his wallet last night.'

'Is he blaming me for that as well?' Chrissie wouldn't put it past him.

'I don't think so,' Ben grinned at her. 'He was up on the Farm Estate, God knows why, unless he's considering buying some land around there.'

'The Farm Estate?' Chrissie repeated. The Forester's Arms was on that estate. Had he gone there expecting to catch her with another man so that he could denounce her to Ben as a cheating trollop? She felt a spurt of anger, followed almost immediately by despair. Why did he hate and distrust her so much? Would it really be so bad if she and Ben were to fall in love and get married?

The anger returned a few moments later when the door opened and Trent Fairfax strode in. Clad in black and with the mark of recent battle on his cheek, he looked extremely sinister. Chrissie forced herself to appear relaxed and glanced at him briefly, disinterestedly, then turned back to Ben.

'Why are you back here?' Ben demanded ungraciously. 'I told you Chrissie was coming at seven.'

'That's probably why he's here – to make sure I haven't fled the country with that flaming ring,' Chrissie said edgily.

'Is that true?' Ben demanded of Trent. 'I thought you were going to look for it?'

'What the hell do you think I've been doing?' Trent asked irritably. 'I've spent most of the afternoon searching your place – you're an untidy young devil, by the way.'

'Have you checked with the management at the Royal Oak?' Ben asked. 'That's where we were on Wednesday night,' he explained, when Trent frowned. 'You're on the wrong track, blaming Chrissie, and I resent it as much as she does,' he added hotly. 'She definitely told me it was too big for her to wear and took it off her finger. After that, I haven't a clue as to what happened to it.'

'Me neither,' Chrissie put in, grateful for Ben's championing of her cause. Trent sighed.

'OK, I'll check with the Royal Oak, but the chances of someone handing it in are pretty slim. It may never be found,' he said, rather bleakly. Chrissie's heart sank: she would be under suspicion for evermore.

'I'm sorry I took it out of the bank,' Ben muttered, half defensively, half apologetically.

'That makes two of us,' Chrissie sighed.

'Three,' Trent corrected. He moved nearer to the bed and studied Ben intently. 'Are you feeling OK? You look worse than you did earlier,' he commented, quite concerned by his brother's pale and perspiring countenance. 'I think I'd better ask the doctor to come and take a look at you.'

Ben looked sheepish. 'Don't do that,' he said quickly. 'I do feel a bit rough, but it has nothing to do with the crash. The thing is, Annabel was here this morning and she left me some Bucks Fizz,' he said, pointing to the now empty bottle innocently proclaiming itself to contain freshly-squeezed orange juice.

'You stupid young fool!' Trent exploded. 'Booze on top of strong painkillers! If you don't grow up pretty damn quick, I'll break that other leg,' he threatened.

'Don't you bully him!' Chrissie jumped to her feet. 'He's feeling rotten.'

'Serves him right,' Trent said callously. 'But I'll still go and have a word with the doctor. And I think you had better leave him to sleep it off,' he added, as he left the room. Chrissie pulled a face at his retreating back, but quickly realized she would have time to slip away while he was busy with the staff, thus saving herself from further interrogation from Torquemada, the Grand Inquisitor. Ben had certainly chosen an apt nickname.

'He does have a point,' she smiled at Ben and picked up her bag. She bent and kissed his cheek. 'I'll come again tomorrow evening.'

'Why not in the afternoon?' he protested. 'You can stay longer.'

'I'll be at work.'

'I thought you were working today?' he grumbled. Chrissie didn't want to get into a discussion as to why she and Sally had swapped shifts.

'Bye, I hope you feel better tomorrow,' she blew another kiss as she left the room. She looked furtively each way along the corridor for a glimpse of Trent, but it was blessedly empty and she ran, negotiated the stairs at a speed an Olympic hurdler would be proud of, and headed out into the car park. Trent's Mercedes was only a few yards away from her Mini, and she huddled low in the seat as she jammed the key in the ignition and stamped her foot on the accelerator. The engine spluttered briefly into life and then died.

'Oh no! Not now, please,' she begged. Desperately she tried again and again, but it refused to start. 'I'll sell you to a scrap yard,' she threatened it, but to no avail. She thumped the steering wheel in frustration, then rested her head on her hands.

'What's wrong?' enquired a voice through her open window; the voice she detested most in the entire world. He sounded amused, Chrissie thought, gritting her teeth.

'My getaway vehicle won't start,' she muttered. 'Go away!'

'That's hardly the way to speak to someone who can give you a lift home,' he remarked.

'I'll phone a garage.'

'On a Saturday night?' he scoffed. 'Come on, Chrissie, don't be silly. I'm on my way to the Royal Oak and I can easily drop you off first.'

'I've got to get the car started; I need it for work tomorrow,' she demurred.

'We have a resident mechanic on the farm; I'll get him out here. Leave the keys under the seat, out of sight,' he instructed. Chrissie still hesitated. But he was right, dammit, she would never get the car fixed tonight without his help. And getting to work on a Sunday by public transport was an absolute nightmare.

'Come along,' he opened the door. Still reluctant, she climbed slowly out, hid the keys as he'd suggested, and silently followed him over to the Mercedes.

She slid into the passenger seat and eyed him rather warily; why was he being so helpful? She was probably in for another interrogation after all, she realized, with an inward sigh.

As he got behind the wheel, she noticed him wince as the edge of the door connected with his bruised cheek. Her spirits rose at once and he gave her a stern look when he caught sight of her grin.

'I bet that's sore – what does the other guy look like?' she asked innocently.

'Guys, plural,' he growled. 'There were two of them and they both look worse than I do.'

'It serves you right for going to the Forester's Arms,' Chrissie said, playing her hunch that he had been looking for her, and not for land suitable for development. He merely grunted by way of reply and her grin broadened: so, her hunch had been right.

'What were you doing there?' she persisted; she wasn't going to let him off so easily.

'Looking after Ben's interests, of course. I've been doing it since before he learned to walk; it's a hard habit to break,' he said, rather ruefully.

'And what would you have done if I *had* been there with another guy?' Chrissie asked curiously.

Hit him, dragged you out, taken you home… Trent thought, before forcing himself to stop following that dangerous path.

'You weren't there, so the problem didn't arise,' he told her smoothly.

He braked for a red light and, as he reached over into the back seat to retrieve his mobile phone, Chrissie shrank back, suddenly made nervous by his proximity. She was reminded of her idiotic behaviour twenty-four hours earlier, when she had assumed, oh so humiliatingly wrongly, that he was going to kiss her, and was determined not to have him believe she was about to repeat the folly. Trent glanced at her sharply, wondering why she was pressed up against the door, and, for a long, silent moment, they stared into each other's eyes.

An impatient tooting from the car behind caused Trent to break the contact. He realized that the lights had changed to green and, with a brief wave of apology to the driver behind, he put the Mercedes into gear and started off. Once moving, the sudden tension eased as quickly as it had arisen.

'I need Jenson's number – he's our mechanic,' he explained. 'I want to make sure that I get hold of him before he goes out for the evening. What time do you have to be at work tomorrow morning?'

'Ten o'clock.'

'Right. Damn, no signal,' he muttered. He had still not got through when he pulled up outside her cottage, and Chrissie reluctantly invited him inside to use her phone. The memory of the night before had her cringing in embarrassment and he was the last person on earth she wanted inside her home, but he *was* doing her a favour, after all.

Once inside, she pointed silently towards the phone and Trent moved past her.

'Would you like a cup of coffee?' she offered unwillingly. She was only being polite and was sure he would refuse, otherwise she would never have asked, and to hell with being polite!

'Thanks. Black, no sugar,' he said, pausing briefly to reply before continuing rattling out instructions to the poor mechanic whose Saturday evening had just been ruined.

Chrissie put the kettle on and stayed in the kitchen, fidgeting unnecessarily with cups, saucers and spoons. She almost dropped a cup when Trent appeared silently at the door and stood there, watching. The kitchen was small; with him in the doorway it became positively claustrophobic.

'He'll get your car started and leave it outside here – assuming it's only a minor problem, of course. I've given him your phone number in case it's something he can't fix.'

'Thank you.' Chrissie poured boiling water on to granules – tough luck if he didn't like instant coffee – and pushed the cup and saucer along the work surface towards him. 'Black, no sugar. Just what Ben needs right now, I expect,' she said brightly, to break the silence. 'Did you talk to his doctor? Will the Bucks Fizz do any damage?' She knew she was babbling and bit the inside of her mouth, hard, to stop herself.

'He'll recover. It could have been a lot worse – neat vodka masquerading as mineral water, for example,' he said dryly. 'I'll have a few words to say to Annabel Harrington-Smyth next time I see her,' he added. Trust her to have a name longer than her skirts, Chrissie thought.

'Is she the snooty blonde who goes around in her underwear?' she asked. Trent smiled: it was a good description.

'That sounds like her. You've met her, then? Do I detect a note of jealousy?'

'No,' Chrissie shook her head.

'No?' he repeated. 'You're very sure of yourself, aren't you? Ben and Annabel have been great friends for years; they practically grew up together.'

'I see,' Chrissie said tightly. 'She's "the right sort", is she? Presumably you wouldn't be making a fuss if Ben had proposed to her?'

'Yes, I would,' Trent surprised her by saying. 'Ben's

immature, totally unsuited for the responsibilities and commitment of marriage.' Privately Chrissie couldn't agree more, but wild horses couldn't have made her admit it, and her chin jutted stubbornly.

'Surely he's old enough to make his own decisions and run his life without interference from you! How old were you when you got married?' she challenged, and ought to have been warned by his sudden frown that she was on dangerous ground.

'Twenty-five,' he said shortly.

'Only a year older than Ben is now,' Chrissie said pointedly. 'But you, I suppose, *were* mature enough for the responsibilities and commitment of marriage?'

'Yes,' he bit out.

'It didn't do you much good, though, did it?' she taunted. 'Maybe if you'd been warmer, more human, your wife might not have...' She got no further. With an exclamation of rage, he slammed down his cup and reached for her with what Chrissie felt sure was murderous intent.

She dropped her own cup and turned blindly towards the back door, hoping to escape into the garden, but he grabbed her, his fingers digging cruelly into her shoulders as he pushed her back against the wall, the hard impact knocking all the breath from her body.

'Don't you dare!' Trent snarled. 'Don't even think of comparing your tacky, money-grabbing relationship with Ben to mine with Francesca!'

'I...I wasn't...' She swallowed nervously, horrified by what she had unleashed, but he wasn't even listening. He was back in the past, she guessed, his thoughts with the wife he had evidently loved very much and apparently still did.

'She was sweet and kind and gentle...' he broke off.

And I never wanted to rip off her clothes the way I want to rip off yours, he was appalled to find himself thinking.

He took his hands from her shoulders and pressed the palms against the wall on either side of her head, but Chrissie didn't even attempt to move away, imprisoned by the hard wall at her back and his body, not touching hers but so close that she could feel the rapid beating of his heart.

He bowed his head, his eyes closed, and Chrissie could see the thick dark lashes fanning his cheeks, watched every tense line in his face as he fought for control. Suddenly, she no longer felt afraid and tentatively put up a hand to touch his cheek. She felt a muscle clench in his jaw as she began gently to caress him, the faint stubble rasping against her fingers.

'Oh, God. Francesca,' he muttered, then raised his head slightly, opened his eyes and looked at Chrissie.

'I'm sorry, so sorry,' she whispered inadequately, swallowing down a lump in her throat at the anguish she saw in the depths of his eyes, at the hurt she had inflicted.

There was no reaction from him, none at all, and she didn't know if he had heard her, or if he even saw her, so she remained immobile as, imitating her own gesture to him, he cupped her cheek in his palm, then rubbed his thumb over her lips, forcing them apart.

This time she knew for sure that he was going to kiss her, but whether he realized who she was she didn't dare contemplate, aware only of a desperate need to assuage his pain, if she could.

He moved to thread his fingers through her hair, holding her captive as he slowly bent his head to hers. She felt his breath warm on her cheek and closed her eyes, beginning to tremble as his lips touched hers, lightly at first, then with a fierce urgency which set every nerve end tingling with a longing she had never experienced before.

She responded hungrily as his hands pulled her to him, moulding her to the hard length of his body. She no longer cared if he thought it was Francesca he held in his arms or if he imagined he was punishing her, Chrissie, by forcing his attentions on her. If this was punishment...

She moaned deep in her throat as his tongue invaded her mouth and a hot ache of desire swept through her body, leaving her weak and clinging helplessly to him. Her hands moved round to caress his back and she pressed closer, feeling her nipples harden as they came into contact with the broad expanse of his chest. She had never known such a wanton need to touch and taste a man; the male scent of him filled her nostrils and inflamed her aroused body even further.

Their clothing was an unwanted barrier and she felt only a wondrous relief and satisfaction when his hands finally slid beneath her sweater to cup her breasts, pushing aside the flimsy material of her bra to tease the already erect nipples and fondle her swollen flesh.

The relief was short-lived, however; soon, she wanted more, much more. She wanted, needed, to have him possess her body, totally and completely. She tried to unfasten the buttons of his shirt, but her shaking fingers were unequal to the task and, with an incoherent sound of impatience, Trent ripped it open and she placed her palms against his heated flesh, curling her fingers into the matt of chest hair before placing her mouth over one nipple in a purely instinctive gesture to give him pleasure.

But then, suddenly and shockingly, he tore himself away from her. Not understanding, Chrissie reached blindly for him, but he flung her roughly aside as if she were a rabid dog – or as if he had just realized who she was, she thought dazedly, able only to watch dumbly as he fastened his shirt and moved to pick up his car keys. Trembling uncontrollably, she leaned against the wall, needing its solid support.

'You just made a big mistake,' he said harshly.

'W-what?'

'I don't think my brother will want you now.' He smiled tightly, evilly. 'Do you?'

chapter five

'Wait!' The sound of her front door being wrenched open with a violence that threatened to take it off its hinges galvanized Chrissie into action and she ran after him. 'Please…'

'Please – what?' He didn't even turn round to look at her. 'Please don't tell Ben? Why not, when that was the object of the exercise,' he said cruelly – and untruthfully; he had no idea what had caused him to behave as he had. But, just maybe, it would solve the problem of the ridiculous engagement. 'I told you earlier – I've been looking out for Ben since he was a baby and I am not going to stand idly by while he makes the biggest mistake of his life…'

'No,' Chrissie couldn't care less about Ben and she couldn't, wouldn't, believe that Trent had felt nothing for her. 'You've got it all wrong. I don't want Ben, I never did,' she said desperately. 'I turned him down. He doesn't make me feel the way you do…'

'Shut up,' Trent snarled at her. 'You can't talk your way out of this one.'

'Trent! Am I …do I look like Francesca?' she asked, as much to her own amazement as his, for she had meant to try to explain how the situation between her and Ben had arisen. Trent half turned and raked her with a glance full of contempt.

'You must be joking,' he said flatly. 'You do not resemble her in any way at all.'

With that last, scathing retort, he headed back to his car and drove off.

Chrissie, moving as stiffly as a very old woman, closed the door behind him and hauled herself wearily up the stairs, clinging on to the banister for much-needed support. Once inside her bedroom, she collapsed in a tearful huddle on to her bed, clutching a pillow for comfort.

Trent only drove a couple of hundred yards, just far enough to be sure he was out of her sight, before he pulled the car over to the side and switched off the engine. How the hell had that happened?

He pushed a wayward lock of hair off his forehead with a hand that shook slightly. He hadn't wanted to make love to a woman so urgently since…since never, he glumly. No wonder Ben was prepared to hand over family heirlooms, if bedding her were the prize… But at least Ben had youth and rampaging hormones as an excuse – I have none, he thought bleakly.

If you seduce her, it will release Ben from this out-rageous engagement, whispered the devil on his shoulder. Yes, but if you *do* get her into bed, could you really tell Ben? Break his heart? whispered the angel on the other.

'Oh hell!' Trent hit the steering wheel hard, then winced. He took a deep breath, then wished he hadn't, for he caught a faint aroma of her scent from his shirt. It was delicate, fragrant – he hated the in-your-face or rather, up-your-nose heavy, cloying perfumes most women favoured. He didn't think Chrissie had been wearing perfume as such, this fragrance was the remnant of shower gel she used, or body lotion perhaps. The mental picture of her applying either to that soft skin and luscious curves made him groan out loud.

'Grow up,' he advised himself. 'She's a sexy little cat out to snare a rich husband. You underestimated her; don't make that mistake again and, for God's sake, remember that it's your job to make sure she doesn't marry Ben!'

He started up the car again and drove to the Royal Oak. It was already crowded so he bought a Scotch and stood at the bar until the staff had a few moments free.

'I'm Trent Fairfax. My brother had a party here on Wednesday night,' he began.

'Yeah, we've got the breakages to prove it.'

'Let me pay for any damages,' Trent smiled pleasantly and pulled out his wallet. He removed several twenty pound notes but hung on to them.

'You'd better speak to the manager,' the barman eyed the twenties greedily. 'Bob? Mr Fairfax would like a word?'

'Yes, sir?' Bob, too, had eyes only for the cash in Trent's hand.

'I understand my brother's party got a little out of hand,' Trent pulled out a few more notes. 'Would a hundred cover any damage?'

'Er, yes, thank you. We were sorry to read in the paper about his accident. Is he going to be all right?'

'Yes, in time. Were you both here on Wednesday night?'

'Yes,' they nodded in unison, eager to answer questions in the hope of further remuneration. Trent was pretty sure his money would go into their pockets and not into the till. But it was not his problem.

'Did you see Ben with a ring? An emerald?'

'No,' Bob shook his head regretfully. 'I didn't, sorry. How about you, Pete?'

'I'm not sure. He was fooling around and went down

on one knee to one of the girls as if he was proposing, but I don't remember an emerald ring.'

'He definitely had the ring with him,' Trent told them. 'But it's gone missing.'

'Oh! I never saw it!' Pete said quickly, afraid he might be blamed for its loss.

'It hasn't been handed in, then? There would be a substantial reward,' Trent said encouragingly. But they both shook their heads. 'Oh well, it was a long shot. Thanks for your time,' he turned to go.

'Excuse me asking, sir,' Bob said quickly, 'but which girl was he proposing to?'

'He wasn't actually proposing; he was only joking,' Trent said swiftly; he didn't want the story doing the rounds if he could help it. 'But what do you mean – which girl?' he frowned.

'Well, there were two of them,' Pete put in. 'Both blondes.'

'Two?' Trent could well believe Ben had been seeing double, but surely not the staff as well?

'Yeah, there was a cute one in a blue dress and another in, well, not much really. See through dress with spangly bits,' Pete said, grinning at the memory.

'Disgusting it was,' Bob tutted disapprovingly. 'My wife wears bigger bikinis.'

'Your wife would need to,' Pete muttered under his breath.

'But surely Ben only offered the ring to one of the girls?' Trent asked.

'Yeah, the one in blue,' Pete seemed positive about that. That must have been Chrissie, Trent thought.

'Nah, surely it was the other one,' Bob demurred. 'He went off with her, anyhow.'

'The one in spangly bits?' Trent frowned slightly. 'You're sure he left here with her? Not the one in blue?'

'Yeah, I'm sure. But, if he was only joking with the other one, I don't suppose it matters, does it?' he asked cheerfully. Trent forced a smile.

'No, it doesn't matter at all,' he agreed. 'Thanks for your help.' He turned and left, and sat in his car for a while, trying to figure out what had happened. It simply didn't add up. Had Chrissie left early and Ben gone home with someone else? That was pretty bizarre behaviour, even for Ben. But, if he had left with another girl…a girl who had wanted the ring for herself? By his own admission, Ben had been too drunk to notice someone rifling his pockets…

Trent picked up his phone to ask Chrissie what she had been wearing on Wednesday, then decided against it. At least, for now. He seemed to lose his mind whenever he was around her. It could wait. Surely Ben would remember soon enough. Sighing, he switched on the engine and headed for Fairfax Hall. First thing Sunday morning he was returning to the sanity of London, he decided grimly.

Chrissie had forgotten to set her alarm clock and was therefore forced to hurry when she awoke late after a restless night, dashing into the bathroom for a quick shower. She daren't let herself think about Trent Fairfax, but couldn't quite banish the memory of his anger, or his passion, even though it seemed that it was Francesca who had aroused it and not her. Even less easy to dismiss was her own answering passion; the strength of it had frightened her at the time, and she was still shocked by the intensity of her emotion and need.

Downstairs, the cottage was redolent of him, a broken cup and spilt coffee testament to what had happened. Ignoring the mess, Chrissie grabbed fruit juice from the fridge, then remembered her car and hurried over to the window. Somewhat to her surprise, for she had half-expected him to instruct his mechanic to tow it to a scrap yard, the Mini was parked outside and, when she looked, she discovered the keys had been pushed through her letter box.

Her mind wasn't on her work at all, although she did vaguely register the presence of Dan Thomson and wonder why he was in the office, for he rarely put in an appearance on a Sunday. Shortly before they were due to close at four, he called her into his office.

'Sit down, Miss Brennan,' he said. That set alarm bells ringing, for he normally called her Chrissie unless his wife was present. That, and his refusal to look her straight in the eye. She knew she'd been distracted all day, but surely she hadn't made some horrendous mistake? She sat, nervously clasping her hands together in her lap.

'I've been checking your contract of employment,' he began, and her stomach lurched in sudden fear. Yet she had done nothing wrong and the current contract had three months to run.

'I'm within my rights to ask you to perform tasks other than your present duties,' he cleared his throat and hoped to hell Trent Fairfax would appreciate this: he was on shaky ground if Chrissie decided to take a case to an industrial tribunal.

'You're not pleased with my work?' she asked slowly.

'It's not that, but I don't see how I can keep you on in the front office, dealing with the public and especially not going into our clients' homes…' He coughed nervously.

'What?' Chrissie wasn't sure she was hearing correctly. Had there been a complaint? But she was meticulous in her behaviour whenever she accompanied would-be buyers, never forgetting that she was a stranger in someone else's home and treating it as she would have hoped others would treat hers.

'Farminster isn't that big a place, Chrissie, and the Fairfax name is well known and respected. There is already talk about a missing ring, and…' He shrugged. 'You can see how I'm placed.'

'You're sacking me?' she whispered.

'No, no,' he denied quickly. 'I want you to work out your contract, naturally, and I'm sure, with a little co-operation on your part, we can find enough work for you, away from the public.'

'Such as what – cleaning?' she bit out. Dan Thomson laughed awkwardly.

'I think we can find something a little more interesting than that. And it won't be for ever.'

'Damn right it won't!' Chrissie said furiously and jumped to her feet. 'You can stuff your contract. I'm quitting, as from now!'

'I think that might be best,' Dan Thomson had got the reaction he had wanted, but he wasn't feeling too good about himself. 'I'll give you an excellent reference, plus the salary to the end of your contract and however much holiday pay you're due,' he said quietly.

Chrissie hesitated: pride dictated she tell him to stuff that, too, but common sense prevailed. She nodded curtly and walked out without another word, head held high. Trent Fairfax was to blame for this, indirectly perhaps, but it was still his fault, she fumed.

Then, on her way through the showroom, she paused,

alerted by the shifty expression on Reg Ford's face and remembered how he had practically rolled out the red carpet for Trent Fairfax on Friday.

'Reg? One question: is Trent Fairfax putting work our…your way?'

'Possibly,' he admitted. Chrissie nodded grimly. Trent Fairfax was to blame, and not as indirectly as she'd thought a moment ago. If you want my business, get rid of Chrissie Brennan. She could almost hear his voice.

Although how she was going to pay the mortgage in a few months was a problem yet to be faced, but back home, she phoned Sally to pour out her woes concerning her job. She kept quiet about making a fool of herself with Trent Fairfax. Again.

'Oh no, that's awful! Poor you. You shouldn't have resigned, though, Chrissie – he didn't have grounds to sack you. Look, I'm coming over,' Sally decided. 'Ten minutes.' She was as good as her word and brought two bottles of wine with her, which Chrissie gladly pounced on.

They had a boozy all-men-are-pigs conversation, blaming Trent Fairfax, Ben Fairfax and Dan Thomson in turn for Chrissie's predicament. Chrissie had forgotten she was supposed to be visiting Ben – the idiot who had started it all – until he called from the hospital to see what had delayed her. Fortunately for Chrissie, Sally picked up the phone.

'No, this is Sally,' she informed him. 'Chrissie can't come to the phone,' she said, correctly interpreting Chrissie's frantic flapping of her hand as meaning she didn't wish to talk to him. 'She's…she's got food poisoning.'

'Men poisoning, more like!' Chrissie snorted.

'Some bug or other…'

'Oh yes, I'm definitely being bugged. By men!' Chrissie interrupted again. Sally frowned and shushed her. 'OK, I'll tell her.' She replaced the handset and looked at Chrissie. 'He hopes you'll feel well enough to visit him tomorrow,' she grinned.

'The selfish sod!' Chrissie muttered. Typical, worrying about how her illness would affect him! 'How did he sound?' she asked, wondering if Trent had told him they had practically ripped each other's clothes off the night before.

'Well, sorry you won't be going to visit him tonight, I suppose,' Sally said, not understanding why Chrissie had asked.

'Sorry as in missing me, or sorry because he's spoiling for a fight?'

'Oh, sorry as in missing you,' Sally decided promptly. Chrissie nodded. Trent hadn't told him, then. It was a pity he couldn't have been similarly discreet with her employer. But of course the loss of the ring didn't reflect badly on him, whereas even Trent would find it difficult to explain away what had happened between them.

Celia was so obviously disappointed when Trent told her of his intention to return to London immediately after breakfast that he relented and promised to stay for lunch.

'But I really must go to the office this afternoon. I was away all day Friday and there will be a pile of papers a mile high on my desk. I can get through it much quicker today, when there'll be no interruptions.'

'You work too hard,' she scolded. 'Why don't we go out riding?' she suggested. 'You hardly ever make the time these days, and Ben's horse will need the exercise.'

'Yes, all right,' he smiled at her. He no longer kept a horse of his own, yet he had always enjoyed riding when he still lived in the country.

They set off at ten, Celia on her grey mare, Fliss, and Trent astride Sultan, Ben's black horse. They trotted companionably side by side, enjoying the fresh cool air with its promise of Spring, and noting the signs of new growth in the flowers and trees as they rode past. Trent matched Sultan's pace to that of the mare, much to the stallion's displeasure as Ben usually gave him his head and allowed him to gallop at breakneck speed across the fields.

'Oh, I forgot to tell you,' Celia said suddenly, 'the police telephoned last night while you were out. Something about a missing ring? The constable said to tell you they haven't located it. I didn't know you'd lost a ring?'

Trent hesitated. 'I haven't. Ben has,' he said shortly. 'He took Grandmother's emerald out of the bank last week.'

'Whatever for? Didn't her will stipulate that the ring was for his future wife?' Celia frowned. Again Trent hesitated.

'Yes.'

'Oh. Annabel, I suppose,' she sighed, not exactly thrilled. She would love grandchildren, of course, but couldn't imagine Annabel providing them. Actually, she couldn't imagine Ben as a husband, either.

'Annabel?' Trent stared at her. Was Ben planning a harem?

'Annabel Harrington-Smyth,' Celia clarified.

'I know who you mean; what I don't understand is why you think Ben proposed to her.'

'Well, because she was here on Wednesday, of course. Or should I say Thursday?'

'*When* was she here?' Trent reined in Sultan and grabbed the mare's bridle.

'I just told you. Wednesday night, but she didn't leave until Thursday morning. She drove Ben home after the party. I know, because I couldn't sleep and I'd just got up to make a milky drink when I heard her car – it's a terribly noisy, open-top sports model. Do you know, she drives around with the top down even in the middle of winter! I told her she'd get chilblains on her nose…'

'Ma!' Trent hung grimly on to his patience. 'Are you sure it was Annabel who brought Ben home after his birthday party?' He spoke slowly and clearly.

'Of course; I've just said so, haven't I?' Celia was a little miffed by his tone. Really, sometimes Trent sounded just like his dear father used to.

'Just Annabel? Or was there a group of people? Perhaps they continued the party at Ben's place?'

'No,' Celia shook her head. 'I looked out of the window. They were making enough noise for a dozen people, but there were only the two of them.'

'And she was still here on Thursday morning?'

'She left about five. Her car woke me up and I looked at my bedside clock.'

'What was she wearing?' Trent asked next. Celia stared at him.

'I couldn't see clearly, but knowing Annabel's taste in party frocks, I suspect she was wearing very little.'

'You didn't notice the colour?'

'No, it *was* dark,' she pointed out. 'Something glittery,' she remembered suddenly. Trent smiled slightly. Annabel was the girl from the Royal Oak, the one wearing the 'spangly bits'. He had already tried to phone Annabel to tear her off a strip for taking alcohol into the hospital, only to be told that she was away for the weekend. Now, he figured her version of events might be worth listening to: if she had been driving, she had, hopefully, been sober enough to remember what had happened, particularly what had happened to the emerald.

He had wondered about Chrissie's phone conversation with Ben shortly before the crash. Now it seemed likely she had been told that Ben had gone home with another girl and they had quarrelled – that would account for her anxious enquiry as to whether he had been upset while driving back to Farminster. It would also explain her assertion that there was no engagement while Ben continued to believe there was. Chrissie had told him to mind his own business when he had questioned her about the call. He'd let it drop at the time, but now he decided that it *was* his business.

'I'm not sure I want Annabel for a daughter-in-law,' Celia said doubtfully.

'Don't worry, Ma. I'm sure it won't happen,' Trent reassured her. 'Come on, I'll race you home.'

Pleading pressure of work – which was true enough – he asked their housekeeper, Molly, to drive Celia in to visit Ben after lunch and set off back to London. Despite his threat to Chrissie, he knew he couldn't tell his brother how she had responded to him. Besides, now he knew Annabel was on the scene, he felt hopeful that Ben wasn't seriously intending to marry Chrissie, and that it therefore wouldn't prove necessary to confess his own, less than honourable action.

On Monday morning, Chrissie set about the depressing task of updating her CV, studying the 'situations vacant' column in the local paper, and checking her finances. She had some savings and, with the promised pay from Thomson and Wilson, should be able to manage carefully for at least six months.

After that...she glanced around her cottage; small certainly, but it was hers. She had enjoyed living here alone for the past two years, revelling in having her own place. Well, hers and the building society's, of course. Perhaps it was because she was an only child, but she hadn't much liked her earlier flat-sharing days. All those petty arguments about who had used up all the hot water, or whose turn it was to put out the rubbish or do the washing up. It had been bliss to put food in the fridge and know it would still be there when she wanted to eat it. And to go to bed at whatever time she chose, secure in the knowledge that she was neither disturbing anyone else nor going to be disturbed by someone coming home in the early hours...

She sighed at the prospect of having to share her space again, but a lodger to help with the bills might be her only answer. Though not yet, she cheered herself. She had a breathing space and should get another job easily enough – if, of course, Trent Fairfax didn't blacken her name all over Farminster. That was a big 'if', she knew, but in that case she might have to cut her losses and leave the town she had lived in all her life.

The key, of course, was locating that ring. Trent Fairfax would have to stop maligning her once it had been found. She made a cup of coffee and sat down to think about it, trying to figure out when and where it could have parted company with Ben's jacket.

Trent was in London, still trying to catch up with his work load and refusing to take any phone calls that weren't urgent.

'I'm sorry, sir, but Dan Thomson from Thomson and Wilson in Farminster is on again,' his secretary informed him. 'This is the third call this morning.'

'Third?' Trent frowned slightly. 'Tell him I'm unavailable,' he said. Dan Thomson was making his eagerness to do a deal too obvious. Let him sweat; the delay would give the man the incentive to shave a few percentage points off the commission he wanted for acting as Trent's agent in the sale of the houses Fairfax Development were building off Tanner Lane. Trent gave a grim smile at the man's persistence to get a contract signed, then promptly forgot about him.

His intercom buzzed again.

'I'm so sorry to disturb you again, sir,' his secretary was sounding nervous, 'but there's a Mrs Harris in Reception, and she insists she needs to see you urgently.'

'Mrs Harris?' Trent queried.

'Your cleaning lady.'

'Oh. Right, you'd better send her in,' he sighed. She had never come to the office building before, so he imagined she had a good reason. He hoped his flat hadn't caught fire or been burgled. 'Mrs Harris,' he stood up as she entered. 'What's wrong?'

'Oh, nothing's wrong, Mr Fairfax, but I thought I'd better come and see you straight away. I was cleaning the spare bedroom and I found this.' She rummaged in her capacious bag and held out the missing emerald ring. 'It looks valuable and, with the plumbers coming in this afternoon, I didn't want to leave it lying around.' She looked at him enquiringly when he didn't answer.

Trent was staring at the ring in disbelief. The bloody thing had been in his own flat the whole time? He had harangued Chrissie, pestered the police who were checking the Porsche, personally turned Ben's place upside down searching for it and, all along, it had been in his own home?

'The spare bedroom? Where Ben rested up last Thursday?' he said heavily. In his mind's eye he could picture Ben entering the room, shrugging off his jacket and tossing it carelessly on to the bed, or even the floor, and later, just as casually picking it up again and not noticing that the ring had fallen from the pocket.

'That's right. Is it Ben's ring?'

'Sort of. When he's twenty five,' Trent said. 'Where exactly was it?'

'It was under the bed. If I hadn't dropped the clean pillow case I might not have spotted it and it could have gone up the vacuum cleaner,' she said. Trent closed his eyes briefly at that thought. One hundred thousand quid lost for ever in the dust-bag.

'Thank you, Mrs Harris,' he said, with heartfelt gratitude.

'I wasn't sure whether to disturb you at your office…'

'I'm very glad that you did,' he smiled at her. 'But you've come miles out of your way,' he realized, and turned to pluck his discarded jacket off the back of his chair. He pulled out his wallet. 'You must take a cab home. And have lunch on me,' he added, peeling off notes. Her eyes widened; the ring must be even more valuable than she'd thought.

'A taxi home would be lovely, Mr Fairfax, but I don't want a reward for honesty,' she said primly. Trent paused; he didn't want to offend her.

'No, of course not,' he said, but folded rather more than she would need for a fare home into her hand. 'Rosa,' he buzzed his secretary. 'Ask the doorman to get a cab for Mrs Harris, please,' he requested and, as he'd thought, that small indication of her importance gave her more pleasure than the offer of cash.

'I'll let you get on with your work,' she beamed at him. Trent nodded, smiled and sat back behind his desk, gazing moodily at the ring in his hand. God, he'd forgotten how big and ugly it was. Had Ben even looked at it? he wondered. If so, hadn't he ever noticed Chrissie's slender, fine-boned hands? Or her colouring? Emeralds wouldn't suit her at all and this particular ring was so big she could probably slide it over her wrist and wear it as a bangle!

The scenes with Chrissie flashed through his mind: he had been so sure she must have kept it. Well, Ben did tell me he was engaged to her, he excused himself, so naturally I assumed his fiancée had the blasted thing! Who else?

But she told you, over and over, that she didn't have it. And you practically threatened to lay criminal charges against her. Just because she's determined to hook a rich husband doesn't mean she'd stoop to stealing what she wants. Lots of women marry money – hell, you've met more than your fair share, but you've never accused any of them of larceny! Chrissie's voice, as clear as if she were in the room, came back to haunt him: 'I'll look forward to hearing your apology!'

Trent reached for the phone, then stilled his hand. He looked at the pile of documents on his desk urgently needing his attention, and sighed heavily. But he knew he had to go and deliver the apology in person. She deserved her little moment of triumph. He picked up his jacket and walked out.

'I'll be gone for the rest of the day.'

'But, sir, your meetings…'

'Re-schedule.' He was already in the lift, stabbing at the button that would get him to the underground car park.

He made better time than he had expected, and reached the outskirts of Farminster late in the afternoon. He glanced at his watch: if he went home first to shower and change out of his city suit, he would still have time to get back into town to meet Chrissie as she left work.

He had decided against calling at her house – it hardly seemed wise, considering he had acted like a lunatic the last time he had been there. No, it was more prudent to meet her at her office and invite her out for a drink. Somewhere public, to ensure they both behaved in a civilized fashion. Well OK, so that's what I'll do, he amended silently. Chrissie would probably accept his apology graciously, if only to make him feel worse than he already did.

He slowed as he neared the turn-off to Fairfax Hall and glanced involuntarily towards the spot where Ben had crashed. The grass verge and fence still bore witness to the ferocity of the impact, but that wasn't what caught his attention. It was a blue Mini, parked off the road, in the middle of nowhere. Chrissie's?

He frowned in perplexity and slowed even more, finally coming to a halt. The Mini was empty – had it broken down again? Where was she? Then he saw her, scrambling up out of the deep ditch and back on to the grass verge. What the…?

Then he realized and a sharp pang of guilt assailed him as he gazed at the forlorn figure; with her shoulders slumped and her head bowed, she was the picture of dejection. His hand closed around the ring in his pocket. She

was searching the crash site for an item that Ben had carelessly left behind in his, Trent's, flat.

Slowly, he climbed out of his car and began walking
towards her.

chapter six

Chrissie had been searching for three hours, but it felt as though she'd been there for three whole days. She was cold, her feet were soaked and she ached in every muscle. This was hopeless! Of course, it would have to be an emerald, blending nicely into the green grass. Why couldn't it have been any other stone, something which might, just possibly, catch the eye?

She had been so full of optimism when she set out, figuring that the ring could easily have fallen, unseen, out of the wrecked Porsche when it was hoisted clear of the roadside. But no, apparently she had guessed wrongly. She had searched every inch, mostly on her hands and knees, and had even dredged the icy-cold, filthy water at the bottom of the ditch with her hands.

And just now, when she had finally thought she had seen a glitter of gold…yuk, she shuddered, almost retching. It had been a rat. Huge, with evil eyes. It had probably eaten the ring.

There was one portion of ditch still to search and she tried to summon up the courage to go back to it. Pretend you're in the SAS, she told herself. Get in quick, do the business and get back out before the enemy knows you're there. That didn't work; her feet remained firmly on the grass verge. OK, so pretend it wasn't a rat, only a water vole. Not that she had the faintest idea of what a water vole looked like, but it sounded far less horrendous than a rat.

She was still giving herself a stern talking-to when she heard footsteps approaching. She had already been propositioned twice, been tooted at several million times and had innumerable – and fortunately inaudible – comments yelled at her by passing lorry drivers. If this creep thought…

'You!' She could hardly believe her eyes. Britain's answer to JR Ewing! 'Just when I thought things couldn't get any worse. What do you want – blood?'

'I've come to apologize,' Trent said quietly, and held out his hand. Chrissie stared in disbelief at the horrible ring lying in his palm. 'It's been in my flat since last Thursday,' he continued.

'In…your *what*…?' Incoherent with rage, Chrissie flew at him. 'You had it all the time!' she accused, pummelling his chest with her fists. Trent stoically did nothing to stop her.

'No…' he began, but she was beyond reason and continued hitting him as she berated him.

'I've been here *all day*!' she cried, feeling a little exaggeration was justified. 'And there are *millions* of rats down there. And an even bigger rat up here!'

'Quite,' Trent agreed gravely. Chrissie narrowed her eyes suspiciously. Was he laughing at her? She renewed her attack with her fists and Trent suppressed a wince. God, she was stronger than she looked. Out of sheer self-preservation, he took hold of her wrists and pulled them down to her sides, holding her captive. The frustration of not being able to hit him enraged her further.

'I hate you!' She twisted in an effort to free herself but he held her firmly.

'I know,' he said quietly.

'You got me sacked! I might have to sell my house! I

suppose you think that will make me leave Farminster?'

'What?' Trent stared down into her furious face, saw the soft glisten of tears in her dark pansy eyes.

'I did not get you sacked,' he denied.

'You did! Dan Thomson knew about the ring and wanted me out of the way, as if I'd got smallpox or something. You told him to get rid of me.'

'I didn't, Chrissie, believe me.'

'Believe you? Hah! Why should I believe you? You never believe a word I say, so why should I believe you?' she demanded, aiming a kick at his shins since he still held her wrists. Trent winced: she had a point.

'I promise I knew nothing about it, Chrissie. If Thomson dismissed you because of rumours about the ring, then I'll put him straight and make sure you're re-instated,' he said earnestly.

'Yeah, sure you will,' she sneered.

'I will. Come on Chrissie, think about it,' he cajoled and made the mistake of trying to lighten the situation with a joke. 'If Ben's going to get married, don't you think I'd prefer it to be to someone who brings home a pay cheque? Don't I have enough dependent relatives already?' He tried a winsome smile; another mistake. Chrissie scowled.

'Not funny!' She kicked him again. Trent almost yelped in pain; God, he'd be black and blue. 'I hate you,' she said again, in case he hadn't got the message yet. 'You called me a thief,' she muttered, swallowing back tears.

'I know; I'm truly sorry.' He held her close and rested his chin on her hair. He was deeply concerned about her losing her job: scotching a rumour once it had started the rounds wouldn't be easy, but he would have to do it.

Physically and emotionally exhausted, Chrissie leaned against him and closed her eyes. Suddenly, she felt calmer, able to cope, as the realization that the wretched thing had been found swept over her.

Neither Trent nor Chrissie heard the screech of brakes as Annabel Harrington-Smyth tore past, saw them embracing and swivelled her head round so fast she almost gave herself whiplash. Trent Fairfax and Chrissie Whatsit! Well, well, – a visit to poor darling Ben was definitely in order, she thought gleefully as she accelerated away.

'I'm OK now,' Chrissie sniffled finally, pulling away from him and searching for a tissue. Trent silently handed her his handkerchief, then held out the emerald. It wasn't his to give, of course, but offering it seemed the least he could do.

'That's the most vulgar piece of jewellery I've ever seen,' Chrissie eyed it with revulsion.

'It's insured for a hundred thousand pounds,' Trent said dryly.

'Big deal!' Chrissie shrugged. God, she was glad she hadn't known that while it was still missing.

'Ben wanted you to have it,' he said, though he knew he would move heaven and earth to prevent a marriage. 'You've earned it,' he said, and knew at once that he had said the wrong thing, yet again.

'Earned it?' Chrissie snarled. And, before either of them realized what she was going to do, she snatched the ring from his hand and hurled it as far away as she could.

Almost before it left her hand, she was horrified by her own action. She watched it while, as if in slow motion, it arced through the air, sailed over the fence – at least it missed the rat-infested ditch, she thought dazedly – and landed somewhere in the field beyond.

She looked apprehensively at Trent and his expression of utter disbelief almost made her burst into hysterical laughter. Then he looked at her, his mouth twitched and her jaw dropped open in shock when he threw back his head and laughed. He wasn't in hysterics, either, she realized; he was actually amused!

'Do the selectors for the English cricket team know about your bowling skills?' he asked, wiping tars of mirth from his eyes. Chrissie blinked.

'I threw the ring away,' she told him, very slowly and clearly. Perhaps he thought she had been pretending.

'I know. But I saw where it landed, near enough. I'll retrieve it later.'

'Shouldn't we get it now?' she asked nervously. It would be just her luck if some nutter with a metal detector came along and claimed it.

'You can if you like, but I am not going into that field,' Trent said firmly.

'Why not? You're not scared of a few cows, are you?' she scoffed.

'No, but I'm not a matador, either. That one peering at us is a bull,' he informed her.

'So? You're not wearing red; you'll be quite safe,' she said airily.

'You're willing to stake my life on that, are you?' he asked, still smiling. Chrissie grinned back, amazed by the transformation in him. He looked younger, carefree.

'Yes!'

'OK, here I go,' he said resignedly. 'But warn me if he looks ready to charge.'

'Of course,' Chrissie agreed, rather too readily. Trent shot her a look of suspicion and she smiled innocently.

'Oh God,' he muttered, but he couldn't back down now.

He negotiated the ditch without falling in, or even getting his feet wet, much to Chrissie's disappointment, for her own feet were like blocks of ice, grabbed on to the wooden fence and hauled himself up and over without any difficulty. He dropped down into the field and, with one eye on the bull and one on the grass beneath his feet, he began searching.

He let out a breath of relief when his groping fingers located it almost immediately, and he snatched it up. The bloody thing was going into the deepest, darkest bank vault he could find!

'Er…Trent? How do I know when the bull's going to charge?' Chrissie asked casually.

'He'll lower his head and start pawing the ground.'

'Er…like that, d'you mean?'

'What?' Trent looked up. '*Oh, Jesus*!' He leaped both sideways and backwards and vaulted the fence all in one fluid movement. Chrissie was impressed. She was also pleased that he landed feet first in about six inches of cold, dank ditch water. He swore fluently under his breath as he clambered back on to the grass verge.

'Did you enjoy your paddle?' she enquired sweetly. He narrowed his eyes at her, but figured she deserved her moment of triumph.

'No, that water's freezing.'

'Yes, I noticed that, too. About three hours ago,' she glared at him.

'We're both cold and wet. What do you say we go and dry off and then have a civilized chat about your job?' he suggested.

'Where?' Chrissie asked cautiously. He waved his arm in the direction of Fairfax Hall, its roof just visible in the distance.

'My mother will be home,' he said quickly. 'She'd enjoy having you come to tea.'

Chrissie glanced uncertainly down at her mud-spattered jeans and shoes.

'I'm not dressed for afternoon tea with your mother,' she objected, more than a little suspicious of his offer. She didn't think Trent Fairfax would invite her to tea simply because he thought she might be thirsty! Which she was, actually, extremely thirsty. And hungry. And desperate to go to the loo. 'I'm scruffy and dirty.'

'So am I, now,' he said dryly. 'Come on, Chrissie. We do have hot water and soap, you know.'

'Oh, all right,' she agreed, won over by the dual arguments of hot water as well as tea. 'I'll follow you in my car.'

'Fine,' he nodded, and went back to where he had parked the Mercedes.

Chrissie climbed into her Mini and trailed after him, along the main road for a short distance and then on to the turning for Fairfax Hall. A long, tree-lined avenue led up to the large, yellow brick building and Chrissie began to feel nervous at the sight of such splendour. However, she pulled up on the gravel alongside the Mercedes and got out.

'I hope you won't feel insulted if we go in the back way,' Trent smiled at her, indicating both his and her own muddy feet.

'No, but are you sure your mother won't mind my being here?' Chrissie asked anxiously.

'Of course not; she loves having visitors,' Trent assured her, putting his hand lightly on her arm to steer her around the side of the house to a large paved courtyard at the rear.

He spotted Celia in the garden room, arranging a bowl of early daffodils and forsythia, and rapped on the window to gain her attention. Celia looked up, startled, then a broad smile lit up her face. She pushed open the window and leaned out.

'Trent! How lovely! I wasn't expecting to see you! And Chrissie… Oh.' The smile vanished, and Chrissie tensed, deciding she was unwelcome here, after all. But that wasn't Celia's concern. 'There's nothing wrong with Ben, is there?' she asked anxiously of Trent.

'No, it's nothing like that,' he assured her quickly. 'Ma, we're both wet and cold – can you look after Chrissie while I go and change?'

'Of course, with pleasure,' she smiled warmly at Chrissie, then bustled off and met them at the kitchen doorway. The room was blissfully warm, with heat positively radiating from the Aga. There was a delicious aroma of baking and Chrissie's stomach rumbled; she had been too uptight and anxious to get on with her search to bother with lunch.

'What on earth have you been doing?' Celia tutted, but didn't wait for an answer. 'Take your shoes off, both of you, before you catch your deaths…do you mind wearing a pair of my socks while yours dry, dear?'

'Not at all,' Chrissie said gratefully.

'I'll be back in five minutes,' Trent said, and disappeared upstairs for a quick shower and change of clothes.

Celia fussed over Chrissie, even tried to insist that she have a hot bath, but Chrissie convinced her she would be fine once she dried off her feet and warmed up in front of the fire.

Trent returned as promptly as promised, looking refreshed and wearing black cords and a thick, white sweater. His lips twitched in amusement when he saw Chrissie's feet, covered in pink socks and matching slippers decorated with teddy bears, but a narrowing of her eyes stilled the comment on his lips.

'Chrissie tells me you've found the ring? I hope it's going back into the bank, wretched thing.'

'It is,' Trent said firmly.

'Good. Come and sit down and have some tea. Victoria sandwich or Eccles cake?'

'Both, please,' Trent said promptly, sitting down beside Chrissie and piling food on to the plate in front of her as well as the one Celia handed to him.

Chrissie sat back, beginning to relax, and gazed around her. The kitchen was large but comfortable, and a pleasing mixture of old and new. Obviously many of the original features had been retained when it was modernized, and functional up-to-date appliances nestled cosily with antique dressers and an assortment of chairs that had seemingly been consigned to the kitchen when they were no longer required elsewhere.

She was thawing out with every passing minute, and tucked into the tea and cakes while Celia prattled happily to Trent, occasionally darting off, still talking, to fetch more goodies from the larder.

'Try some of these biscuits,' she urged Chrissie. 'They're home-made.'

'Ma, you're a fraud,' Trent scolded lightly, reaching across Chrissie for a handful of chocolate-chip cookies. 'Molly, our housekeeper, baked these,' he explained, through a mouthful of crumbs.

'They're still home-made,' Celia declared.

'Of course they are,' Chrissie agreed with her.

'Do you enjoy cooking, Chrissie?' Celia asked her. 'Oh, I suppose you don't have much time, working as you do,' she answered her own question, a trait Chrissie was quickly becoming familiar with. She rather suspected it had become a habit because Trent and Ben rarely answered their mother's questions.

'Is today your day off?' Celia enquired brightly.

'Er…no,' Chrissie shot a look at Trent. 'Actually, I've lost my job.'

'Oh dear! Not because you dashed off last week to visit Ben in hospital?'

'No. Unfortunately, my boss heard about the missing ring,' Chrissie shrugged.

'How? No one knew about it, except the family…'

'Mmm,' Chrissie stared steadily and accusingly at Trent. He shook his head in denial.

'Oh, the police knew…' Celia said, frowning. 'But surely, they…'

'The staff at the Royal Oak knew,' Trent put in. 'Truly, Chrissie, Thomson did not hear about it from me.'

'You know him, Trent? Can't you do something to help?' Celia asked anxiously.

'Don't worry, Ma, I intend to,' he assured her, then turned to Chrissie. 'I'm assuming you do want your job back? If not, I'd say you have a pretty good case for constructive dismissal.'

'Go after cash I haven't earned, you mean?' Chrissie asked tightly. Trent grimaced: obviously he had said the wrong thing. Again. 'In that case, perhaps I should sue you for slander,' she added thoughtfully. Trent decided to ignore that.

'Employment laws exist to protect workers from bosses like Dan Thomson,' he said quickly. 'I have a lawyer on retainer to…'

'To protect your workers?' Chrissie asked, feigning wide-eyed innocence. Trent grinned.

'No, to protect me,' he admitted. 'But…'

'More tea?' Celia interrupted, not liking the change in atmosphere. 'Don't worry, dear, Trent will sort it out,' she said soothingly. Suddenly, Chrissie's annoyance melted: she had a feeling both Celia and Ben relied on Trent to sort things out on a regular basis.

'No, thank you,' she declined the offer of more tea. 'I really ought to go.'

'Not yet,' Trent said quickly. Both women looked at him questioningly. 'If you don't mind, Chrissie, I'd like to ask you a few questions about what went on at Ben's party,' he said, carefully polite. But evidently not politely enough.

'Oh, not again!' she said crossly. 'You've got the ring back – what more do you want?'

'Is that the phone?' Celia tilted her head to listen to non-existent ringing. 'Molly's out; I'll answer it,' she said and hurried out of the room. She didn't go far, though, just far enough to be out of sight, not out of earshot. Trent and Chrissie barely noticed her leave. Then Trent leaned closer to Chrissie.

'That look of defiance would be more effective if you weren't wearing my mother's fluffy pink slippers,' he said softly, a grin tugging at the corners of his mouth and blue eyes twinkling.

'Oh!' Chrissie glanced down at her feet. 'Aren't my socks and shoes dry yet?'

'I'll check.' He reached down and prodded the shoes leaning against the stove and then handed them over. 'Here you are.'

'Thanks.' Chrissie pulled them on, then, 'What did you want to ask me?'

'Not here.' Trent knew his mother too well. 'Do you like horses? Would you like to come and see ours?'

'Yes.' Chrissie stood up and shrugged on her jacket. Trent found a warm sheepskin coat hanging in the rear lobby and put it on. As he opened the back door, a black and white collie bounded in and leaped joyously up at him.

'Hello, boy. This is Oscar,' he told Chrissie.

'Hi, Oscar,' she put out a hand and he sniffed at her, then wagged his tail in apparent approval. 'Is he yours?'

'No, Ben's. I expect he's been waiting at Ben's place. Ma keeps bringing him over here, but every time she lets him outside, he dashes over to see if Ben's back yet,' he explained.

'Aah, poor Oscar,' Chrissie patted him sympathetically. 'Where exactly *is* Ben's place?'

'Haven't you seen it?' Trent was surprised.

'No.'

'I was pretty sure that he'd invited you,' Trent persisted. Chrissie looked at him sharply, but he was smiling.

'Yes, he did,' she admitted, 'But…let's just say it didn't seem like a good idea.'

'You thought he'd pounce,' Trent translated correctly.

'No comment,' Chrissie said lightly, feeling they were heading for dangerous ground. 'What do you want to talk to me about?' she asked again.

'I'd like to hear everything that happened at Ben's party,' he replied.

'Everything? Even the stripper?' she grinned, and he laughed out loud.

'Especially the stripper,' he said firmly, and closed the door behind them.

Celia stepped back into the kitchen and absently fussed Oscar while her thoughts raced. She hadn't realized just how long it had been since she had heard her elder son laugh like that. The carefree sound had almost shocked her, so alien was it. Not since the early days with Francesca, she thought, and she had always had her doubts about the marriage. Francesca had been a sweet girl, of course, just not right for Trent. There had been no fire, no spark…

She hurried over to the kitchen window and peered out. Trent had one hand at Chrissie's waist as he steered her across the courtyard towards the stable block. I mustn't meddle, Celia told herself firmly, even while her mind was busily working out what she could do to help things along.

She scarcely gave Ben a thought: Annabel Harrington-Smyth would be ample compensation, as her presence until the early hours on Thursday morning testified. Besides, Ben didn't have a serious bone in his body; he was happy-go-lucky, always had been and would be again once his injuries had healed, eager for the next diversion life had to offer.

No, it was Trent who really needed to be healed, Trent who had the deepest wounds, and just possibly Chrissie Brennan was the girl to perform the miracle. Celia had noticed on Friday, at the hospital and in the car, and again today over tea, how intently Trent watched Chrissie. And Chrissie watched him, too, rather warily, it had to be said, but also with fascination. Celia hadn't been to a church service since the day her husband had died, so young and senselessly, but she offered up a prayer now.

'That's Ben's,' Trent pointed to the glass-fronted building at one end of the courtyard. 'It was once part of the stable block, but we only keep two horses now.' He pushed open the door and ushered her in to the stable. It was warm and snug, and the two horses poked their noses over the stalls to see who was visiting.

'This is Fliss, she belongs to Ma,' he said, scratching the mare's ears before delving into a nearby bin for carrot and apple. 'And this is Sultan – he's Ben's,' he introduced the stallion. He seemed massive in the confines of the stable and Chrissie prudently decided to remain beside the mare. 'Do you ride?' Trent asked.

'I can do, sort of, but I haven't for years.' She hesitated, then, 'Charles Hawksworth taught me,' she added.

'I see.' Trent's lips tightened at the mention of her former boyfriend. What else had he taught her? But he had caught the tentative note in her voice and knew she wasn't taunting him with the information. She hadn't had to tell him; it was almost as if she didn't want to keep it a secret from him. He relaxed and handed her some treats to feed to Fliss.

'Tell me about Wednesday evening,' he prompted quietly. 'But first – you were wearing a blue dress – right?'

'Right,' Chrissie stared at him in perplexity – what had that to do with anything? – then shrugged slightly. There was a calm and peaceful atmosphere in the stable, with the two horses munching placidly.

'It was a nightmare, actually,' she began frankly. 'I felt out of place, right from the time I arrived, possibly because almost everyone else was drunk. The…proposal took me totally by surprise. It came out of nowhere; I had absolutely no idea he was even thinking along those lines. But suddenly he produced that horrible ring and was going on about how he wanted to look after me…' She cleared her throat uncomfortably. 'I'm certain that he'd never got as far as thinking about marriage, he just hoped an engagement would… er…' She stopped.

'Get you into bed?' Trent supplied, concentrating hard on fussing Sultan. For once in his life, he was fully able to understand Ben's behaviour.

'Well, yes,' Chrissie's cheeks flamed. 'I told him not to be so silly, and put the ring back in his pocket. Then the stripper arrived and I didn't hang about much longer. Ben was fooling around with a couple of his friends and I'm sure he didn't notice me leave,' she added dryly.

Trent didn't reply; he couldn't trust his motives in telling her that Annabel Harrington-Smyth had accompanied Ben home and, more importantly, had stayed until the early hours.

'You know the rest,' Chrissie continued after a moment. 'I was going to talk to Ben when he sobered up, but he went off to London to see you. He phoned me when he was on the way back and I told him I wouldn't marry him. He was…abusive,' she said, and Trent looked up sharply, 'so much so that I told him I didn't even want to see him any more. But then he crashed the car and wanted to see me. He seems to have forgotten that last conversation we had,' she sighed. 'But I suppose that's only temporary. I'm just glad you found the ring. And I'm sorry I hit you,' she said, but rather spoiled the apology with a grin she couldn't quite hide.

'You kicked me as well,' he growled, turning to look at her. Her blonde hair gleamed softly in the dimness of the stable and her face, devoid of make-up, bore a smudge of dirt she had missed when cleaning up earlier. In jeans and denim jacket she looked about sixteen. Which was disturbing, because she also looked utterly desirable.

'Sorry!' Again, there was the impish grin and Trent had to summon up every ounce of willpower he possessed to stop himself grabbing her and kissing her, carrying her over to the pile of hay and…

chapter seven

'Trent!' It was Celia calling, and he swore under his breath.

'In here,' he moved to open the door.

'I've just had a wonderful idea.' She beamed.

'Oh God!' Trent muttered.

'Don't be rude – I *do* have good ideas occasionally,' she reproved him. 'It's about this horrid rumour that Chrissie's employer obviously got wind of. Well, I know what we can do to stop it going any further!' she said, thoroughly pleased with herself. 'You see, I've got tickets for a charity fashion show at the Park Hotel this evening – I wasn't going to attend, I only bought the tickets because the proceeds go to the local hospice…'

'Ma,' Trent tried to stem the flow. 'What does this have to do with helping Chrissie?'

'I was telling you; don't interrupt. The Press will be there – only the local papers, of course, but they always print loads of photographs, and Chrissie's so pretty…I *am* getting to the point,' she said, noting that Trent looked ready to explode while Chrissie looked merely bemused. 'Everyone we know will be there, too, and if Chrissie's with me, as my guest, it will stop any more nasty gossip, won't it?' she finished triumphantly.

'Well,' Trent said thoughtfully, and glanced at Chrissie to gauge her reaction. 'It's not a bad idea,' he conceded, and Chrissie nodded her agreement.

'I think Ben will be expecting to see me tonight,

though,' she demurred.

'He won't mind,' Celia said quickly. 'And you'll be staying here overnight, won't you, Trent? So you can visit Ben,' she added. Trent nodded: he had intended to anyway, to try to discover what the young devil was playing at with Annabel Harrington-Smyth.

'Sure,' he agreed.

'But can you drop us off at the hotel and pick us up later?' Celia asked him.

'That won't be necessary,' Chrissie put in. 'I can do the driving.'

'Oh no, dear, Trent has to do that,' Celia contradicted quickly. 'People think I'm a scatty old biddy, but everyone knows Trent wouldn't be taken in by…by a…' she faltered.

'By a gold-digger?' Chrissie asked, shooting a glance at Trent. 'A thief, even?'

'No one ever thought that, dear,' Celia denied hastily. 'But I *do* think it would be best for you to be seen as a friend of the family, not just one of Ben's…friends,' she finished lamely.

'I don't mind driving you both,' Trent said, and looked over at Chrissie. 'You'll want to go home and change first, won't you, and then you'd have to trek back out here again. What time does this shindig start, Ma?'

'Seven thirty.'

'Right.' Trent checked his watch. 'We'll collect you at seven fifteen?' he raised an eyebrow at Chrissie.

'Fine,' she agreed. She wasn't sure a public appearance would help all that much, but it certainly couldn't do any harm. And it was very kind of Celia to have suggested it. 'Thanks. And thank you for asking me,' she added to Celia.

'My pleasure, dear. I'm such a nuisance, not being able to drive.'

'Have you never had lessons?'

'Oh yes, loads,' she said happily. 'My dear husband tried to teach me and then Trent did, too, but they both shouted…so then I had lessons from a proper teacher,' she said, with a reproving look for Trent. 'He was ever such a nice man, and so helpful, and he never shouted, not once…'

'He didn't get you through your test, either,' Trent pointed out. 'Excuse me, but I need to phone the office. I'll see you later, Chrissie,' he nodded to her and began walking back to the house.

'Is your car at the front, dear? I'll walk round with you.'

'How many times did you take the driving test?' Chrissie asked.

'Twice,' Celia said, then, as Chrissie was about to assure her lots of people needed more than two tests, Celia lowered her voice. 'Actually, dear, I failed it five times before I decided to give up. But don't tell the boys – you know what they're like on the subject of women drivers.'

'I won't tell them,' Chrissie promised. She was still smiling as she drove away. The boys. She could just picture the look of disgust on Trent's face if he knew his mother referred to him in such a way. She was becoming very fond of Celia Fairfax.

The Park Hotel was the best in Farminster, and Chrissie dressed accordingly, choosing one of her smartest outfits, a powder-blue skirt and jacket with fake fur collar which she had bought for a friend's wedding, a few months before.

Celia had said 'everyone' would be there, meaning,

presumably, anyone in the district who had money. No doubt the clothes on show would be hideously expensive, or maybe just plain hideous – old lady clothes in floral patterns and with elasticised waists, but, despite that, Chrissie found she was quite looking forward to the evening. Perhaps it was just the sheer relief of the emerald ring being found, but, for now at least, not even the loss of her job was worrying her.

She was watching out for Trent and Celia from her bedroom window, and ran down the stairs as soon as she spotted the Mercedes turn into her road.

Celia very much approved of the suit and stole a look at her son to see if he did, too. However, in the semi-darkness she could make out no discernible expression on his face. He got out to open the passenger door for Chrissie, but, beyond a murmured 'Good Evening', he made no comment.

But Celia took heart from the realization that Trent had already known exactly where Chrissie lived – he hadn't needed to ask for her address or for directions on how to find the house.

'How lovely you look, Chrissie,' she said warmly, but decided she would be pushing her luck if she tried to prompt a compliment from Trent. 'And what a lovely house,' she added, with a note of surprise.

'Well, thank you,' Chrissie was a little taken aback. 'It's very small, but I think it has a lot of character.'

'It seems quite large… Oh!' Celia realized her mistake when she noticed fences and three more front doors. 'You don't live in all of it…'

'Just the end cottage, Number Two,' Chrissie told her calmly.

'But how nice, having so many near neighbours,' Celia

tried her best to retrieve the situation, but only succeeded in making it worse with every word. 'We're so isolated at the Hall and it's far too big. Mostly I'm there alone, apart from the staff of course, and it's so cold in winter. I spend most of the time positively huddled over a fire in the smallest room…'

'Ma, shut up,' Trent said, but quite gently. He looked at Chrissie through his rear-view mirror and smiled ruefully. 'The words foot and mouth spring to mind, don't they?'

'Oh no!' Celia put a hand to her mouth. 'I hadn't heard about another outbreak! We had to slaughter hundreds of cattle last time, and…'

'Mother!'

'I'll shut up,' she said meekly.

The car park at the hotel was already full, and Trent dropped them off at the entrance.

'Tell Ben I'll be in to see him tomorrow,' Celia said to Trent. 'And be sure to ask if he needs anything. And…'

'What time shall I pick you up?' he interrupted.

'Oh, about nine-thirty? Come inside and say "Hello" to everyone, won't you? It would be a good idea if they all saw you and Chrissie having a drink together.'

'Fine. Enjoy yourselves.'

'We will.' Celia tucked her hand into the crook of Chrissie's arm and they walked up the steps to the glass doors which a uniformed doorman opened for them. Several waiters were hovering in the foyer, offering complimentary glasses of champagne. Celia took two and handed one to Chrissie, waved at a couple of her cronies before spotting her real target – a photographer.

'Young man,' she beckoned imperiously. 'I'm Celia Fairfax and this is Chrissie Brennan,' she told him. She so obviously expected to have her photograph taken that he obliged immediately, taking several shots before she was satisfied.

'Thank you,' Celia smiled graciously, then drew Chrissie forward to greet some of her friends. 'Suzy! Davina! How lovely to see you! Have you met Chrissie Brennan?' She continued to introduce Chrissie to all and sundry until they were invited to move into the conference room where the fashion show was to take place.

A T-shaped catwalk had been set up in the centre of the room, with rows of spindly gilt-framed chairs arranged around it so that everyone would have a clear view.

'Celia, darling!' Fiona Harrington-Smyth took a seat behind them, leaned forward to exchange an air kiss with Celia and glanced curiously at Chrissie. 'Chrissie Brennan?'

'That's right,' Celia smiled.

'The name sounds familiar…I know, Annabel was telling me something about Ben – of all unlikely people – proposing! I didn't believe it, but – is it true?'

'No, Chrissie and Ben are friends, nothing more,' Celia said firmly. 'They were playing a prank on the others, but it seems to have got rather out of hand! You never imagined it would cause this much gossip, did you, Chrissie dear?'

'No,' she agreed.

'Oh! So Ben didn't have his grandmother's emerald ring?' Fiona sounded disappointed.

'Of course not. Trent would have a fit if Ben removed that from the bank,' Celia said. Which was true enough, Chrissie thought, exchanging a warm smile with Celia. She had underestimated the older woman. Celia had just killed two birds with one stone; denying with one short conversation both the rumour concerning the engagement, and that concerning the loss of a valuable ring.

'Fiona Harrington-Smyth is a dreadful old gossip,' Celia whispered to Chrissie. 'Telling her will prove more effective than taking out a full page advertisement in *The Times*! Oh, here's Annabel, late as usual…'

Annabel was late because she'd simply had to go to the hospital to tell Ben that she had seen Trent kissing Chrissie. She almost wished she hadn't bothered; Ben had been in a foul mood before she'd told him, and positively suicidal afterwards. No fun at all!

Then to make matters even worse, she had bumped into Trent Fairfax – devastatingly attractive, of course, but boy, did he need to lighten up – and he had actually reprimanded her, in public and as if she were a child, for taking poor Ben champagne.

'Apparently Ben Fairfax was playing a joke with that engagement business,' Fiona whispered to her daughter when she sat down. 'I've just heard it straight from Celia.'

'Let's hope she's got it right for once. God, what's *she* doing here?' she had just noticed Chrissie. 'She can't afford any of the clothes here,' she added loudly. Chrissie was faintly amused, but Celia was outraged. Really, how ill-bred! Fiona ought to do something about her spoilt daughter, she fumed, unaware that popular opinion said much the same about her and her younger son.

'The most expensive item is always the wedding dress at the end,' she told Chrissie. 'Shall we put her nose out of joint and buy it?' she asked longingly. Chrissie laughed and shook her head.

'Are all the clothes for sale?'

'Yes, and all the proceeds go to the hospice. Many of the local shops donate garments and accessories, too.'

'I see.' Chrissie settled back to watch the show. It was

certainly aimed at a wealthy audience, but her fears about it being only suitable for matrons were unfounded. Which in a way was a pity, because Annabel was quite right – Chrissie couldn't afford the clothes she liked. Even if she hadn't just lost her job, she would have thought long and hard about paying so much money for clothes.

Celia, usually the most easy-going of people, became very distressed as Annabel flashed her credit card incessantly and tried to provoke Chrissie into doing the same.

'It *is* for charity, after all. One has to do one's bit – *noblesse oblige*, you know…well no, perhaps you don't,' she drawled insultingly.

'Annabel!' Celia had to intervene: the only 'obliging' Annabel ever did was for men. 'I hate to say this, really I do, but you are the most frightful snob! And a…bitch!' she finally managed to say a word she rarely used unless discussing puppies. Chrissie's jaw dropped, as did Annabel's and her mother's. Celia felt quite liberated by her outburst and smiled serenely.

'Come along, Chrissie, Trent will be waiting for you,' she said loudly.

'Trent?' Fiona looked at her daughter. 'Surely not?'

'Of course not. Celia Fairfax has lost her mind,' Annabel sniffed. But she wasn't as sure as she hoped she sounded.

After his brief but sharp conversation with Annabel, Trent hurried into the hospital and entered Ben's room without knocking. If the young fool was swigging back more smuggled booze, he wanted to catch him in the act.

'Oh no, you're all I need,' Ben scowled.

'It's nice to see you, too,' Trent retorted, unaware that Annabel had seen him holding Chrissie that afternoon and, of course, equally unaware that she had embellished the tale somewhat. In her version, Trent and Chrissie had been locked in a passionate embrace. 'Have you got any alcohol hidden in here?'

'No!' Ben snapped, but Trent checked anyway, opening and sniffing the contents of the bottles on his bedside locker. Ben glowered at him. It wasn't fair. Trent had everything; the power, the money, and now he was after Chrissie! So much for family loyalty!

'The ring's been found at my flat,' Trent told him. 'It must have fallen out of your jacket while you were there last Thursday.'

'Big deal,' Ben muttered.

'I'm putting it back in the bank tomorrow,' Trent continued. Ben didn't even answer that, just stared sullenly at his brother.

'Why are you in such a bad mood?'

'How many reasons do you want?' Ben snarled. 'I'm stuck in here, in pain and bored to tears. I thought I'd be up on crutches soon, but that's out until the ribs heal. And, even when I am allowed out of bed, I'm going to be confined to a wheelchair…'

'Stop whining!' Trent said sharply. 'You're here through your own stupidity. There was nothing wrong with your car and no other vehicle was involved. The roads weren't icy and it wasn't foggy – the police say the accident was caused by driver error. That means you, Ben. You could have been killed, or killed or maimed some other poor devil. Count yourself lucky you don't have that on your conscience, and that you won't be in a wheelchair permanently.'

'Thanks for the sympathy,' Ben muttered.

'I'm sure you're getting more sympathy than you

deserve from Ma. And Annabel Harrington-Smyth. I saw her on my way in,' Trent said, then paused and watched Ben closely. 'So, what's going on, Ben? You proposed to Chrissie Brennan on Wednesday night, came to my office on Thursday to tell me you're engaged, yet, in between those two events, you spent five hours alone with Annabel.'

'So?'

'So, it's unusual, to say the least. Just which one of them are you stringing along? Were you serious when you proposed to Chrissie, or was it a ploy to get her into bed?' Wouldn't you like to know, brother, Ben thought maliciously. How dare he lecture anyone on how to behave when he was sniffing after his own brother's girlfriend while the said brother was in hospital?

'Of course I was serious,' he stared at Trent.

'She turned you down. That's why you went home with Annabel. Isn't it?' Trent demanded.

'Chrissie didn't turn me down exactly,' Ben shrugged. 'She's playing hard to get; she was embarrassed because I asked her in public, and annoyed because I'd had a few drinks to bolster my courage. She'll say yes next time I ask her,' he said, and watched Trent's mouth tighten. That hurts, does it Trent? he thought.

'Why ask her again? You don't love her, or you'd have gone after her on Wednesday and you certainly wouldn't have spent the night with Annabel. And Chrissie doesn't love you; she's after money,' he said harshly. 'You do know she's the girl Charles Hawksworth was involved with before his father packed him off to Australia?'

'No, I didn't, but so what?' Ben asked carelessly. 'That was years ago.'

'It doesn't worry you that she's determined to get a rich husband?'

'Not really, no. If I'd been born poor, I daresay I'd have wanted to marry money. But that doesn't mean I'd have got hitched to some rich old bag I didn't fancy. The money might be an attraction, but only part of it,' he said, then inspiration struck.

'After all, if money was her main priority, she'd be turning her attention to you now that she's met you. She knows I'm a pauper compared to you,' he said, and knew the deliberately chosen words had hit home. Trent, always mistrustful, would not now believe a word Chrissie said and would be suspicious if she responded to any sexual overture he made.

'She'd be wasting her time,' Trent said harshly. 'I'll never marry her. Or anyone else.'

'Fine. That's your decision. Leave me to make mine,' Ben told him. 'Your days of cracking the whip are nearly over anyway. There's nothing you can do to stop me getting my trust fund when I'm twenty-five, and, in the meantime, I'm sure I could borrow against it if I have to. What makes you think you know what's best for everyone, anyhow?' he went on. 'OK, you've made a lot of money, but you're not happy, are you? You make my life a misery just because I refuse to work as hard as you do. And Ma's, treating her like a kid, doling out pocket money. And Francesca... Sorry,' he muttered, catching the expression of mingled fury and pain on Trent's face and feeling ashamed. 'That was below the belt. I'm sorry.'

A long, tense silence fell between them, broken only when two of Ben's cronies from the rugby club came noisily into the room. Trent said Hello, confiscated the beer they had brought for Ben, said goodbye and left the room.

Before he had even closed the door behind him, he heard Ben laughing and joking, his voice lighter and obviously his spirits, too. The sullen hostility and self-pity had vanished as soon as Trent had.

Perhaps I *am* too harsh? Trent thought, but, if he hadn't been, they would all have been in the bankruptcy court long ago. The tenanted farms no longer kept the estate profitable; the property company had been subsidizing it for years, and that had almost gone under during the last recession.

It was too early to collect his mother and Chrissie from the hotel, so he sat in his car and drank one of the confiscated beers.

He was shaken by the bitter condemnation from Ben: the hero worship had turned to resentment after their father's death, when Trent's role had of necessity become more paternal than fraternal, and therefore often confrontational, but he had never even guessed at the deep-rooted anger which Ben had just displayed.

As for what he had said concerning Chrissie...well, that had only confirmed his own suspicions. So why was it bothering him so much?

He didn't feel inclined to make small talk with his mother's cronies, so he stayed in the car and asked the doorman to convey a message to Celia. She and Chrissie appeared almost at once. Celia opened the door of the front passenger seat but didn't get in.

'You were supposed to come in for a drink and mingle,' she scolded him. 'But we've done a brilliant exercise in...what do they call it? Damage limitation,' she beamed, proud of herself.

'Good.' Trent forced a smile. 'Get in the car, it's freezing.'

'Oh, I'm not coming with you, dear. Judith Lawford will bring me home later. We need to discuss…something,' she said vaguely. 'You take Chrissie home and I'll see you later. Get in, dear,' she urged Chrissie forward. 'How was Ben tonight?' she asked Trent.

'Fine,' he said lightly, not wanting to upset her with the truth. 'The Delancey brothers arrived as I was leaving.'

'Oh good, I'm glad he's got company. Well, goodbye, dear,' she kissed Chrissie's cheek. 'Thank you for coming with me; I really enjoyed myself. I hope I shall see you again, very soon.'

'Thank you for inviting me,' Chrissie smiled shyly, touched by her kindness and warmth.

She climbed into the car and stole a look at Trent. He didn't glance at her or say a word. In fact, he looked as cold and unapproachable as he had the day he had stormed into the office.

'Is anything…wrong?' she ventured, when the silence became oppressive. She thought he was going to ignore her, so long did he take to reply, yet eventually he spared her a brief glance.

'I didn't say anything to my Mother, but Ben was in a pretty bad way. Not physically so much, but he's depressed, angry. I've never known him be so down.' Or so vindictive, he added silently.

'Oh dear. I suppose time drags for him in hospital. He's used to dashing about all day and most of the night,' Chrissie said. 'He's very sporty, too, as well as being a party animal.'

'Yes, I know,' Trent nodded. Perhaps Ben had merely needed to lash out at someone, anyone, in his frustration and he, Trent, had been the unlucky recipient. Better me than Ma, he thought.

'I'm going to try and get him out of hospital as soon as possible,' Trent continued. 'Even if it means having a full-time nurse. He'll still be immobile, of course, there's nothing I can do about that, but at least he'd be at home and his friends can visit at any time.'

'I'm sure he'd cheer up at home,' Chrissie smiled. 'That's very kind of you.'

'Not kind,' he contradicted, and gave a small smile. 'Guilty, I'm afraid. I was a bit rough on him.'

'Why? He hadn't been mixing painkillers and booze again, had he?'

'Not as far as I know. He was feeling sorry for himself and I told him he had no one but himself to blame for what happened to him.'

'Oh,' Chrissie grimaced slightly.

'Too harsh?' he asked.

'N-no,' she said, a little doubtfully. 'I'm sure you're right, but it probably wasn't very…tactful to say so right now.'

'Hmm.' Trent grunted non-commitally and lapsed into silence again.

'Your mother was wonderful tonight,' Chrissie tried another tack.

'Oh? In what way?'

'She gave Annabel Harrington-Smyth a piece of her mind…'

'Oh dear, I'm not sure she can spare it,' he cut in, but he was smiling.

'Trent!' Chrissie laughed.

'I know, it was out of order,' he agreed. 'What did she say to Annabel?'

'She told her she's a snob. And a bitch.'

'Really?' He was surprised. 'What on earth did Annabel

do to incur Ma's wrath?'

'Oh, she was buying everything in sight – in the name of supporting the hospice, of course – and trying to make me look bad because I couldn't afford anything,' she said, lightly and unthinkingly. She wasn't looking at Trent as she spoke, but she saw his hands tighten on the steering wheel and knew precisely what expression would be on his face if she dared to look.

'Never mind, Chrissie,' he said softly. 'I have no doubt but that you'll achieve your ambition of snaring a rich husband one day, and then you'll have as much money to spend as Annabel.' Chrissie bit her lip.

'I…I thought you'd changed your opinion of me since finding the emerald,' she whispered.

'I was wrong about the ring,' he acknowledged. 'And I've apologized. I am also truly sorry you've lost your job and I'll put that right. But,' he braked to a halt outside her cottage, unclipped his seat belt and turned to face her. 'I haven't changed my mind about your relationship with Ben.' He reached out and rubbed his thumb over her mouth. Chrissie stared at him, mesmerized.

'You wouldn't have responded to me the way you did if…' he paused, unbuckling her seat belt and resting his hand lightly on her waist. '…if you were in love with him.'

'I…I'm not!' Chrissie finally managed to speak. A fleeting smile tugged at the corners of his mouth.

'Not what? Not in love with Ben? Or not responsive to me when I do this…?' he touched his mouth to hers. 'Or when I do…this…?' he murmured, trailing butterfly kisses down the column of her throat.

Chrissie's voice of reason, telling her this was a very bad idea, became more and more distant until she could no longer hear it. With a soft whimper of surrender, she arched her neck back, unconsciously thrusting her breasts forwards. Her hands crept up his arms and around his neck, pulling him closer to her while tangling her fingers in the soft dark hair at his nape.

Trent swiftly unbuttoned her jacket and slipped his hands inside, tugging at her camisole top to grant him access to the soft naked skin beneath. Chrissie moaned, deep in her throat, and his hands slid round to her buttocks, lifting her off the seat until she was half-lying across his lap.

The heel of Chrissie's shoe stabbed on the stereo and the sudden blare of music startled them both into laughter. Then a neighbour of Chrissie's, walking her dog, shone her torch into the car and brought Chrissie down to earth with a bump.

She hastily straightened her clothes and sat back in her seat, but she didn't get out of the car, as any sensible girl would do. Or so the voice of reason tried to tell her. Chrissie didn't want to listen and closed her ears to it.

But cool reason wouldn't go away. *He thinks you're a good time girl out to catch a rich husband – and about as welcome in his family as King Herod in a maternity ward*! Chrissie tried her best to ignore it; the voice she wanted to hear was Trent's, deep and husky. And she didn't want to go into her cottage, alone. She wanted to feel Trent's hands and mouth on her body.

Trent interpreted the signs of desire correctly. But accustomed as he was to bedding sexually experienced women and wrongly assuming that Chrissie was one of them, he made a rare error.

'Your neighbour is still watching us,' he murmured. 'Tongues will wag if my car is here all night. Shall we go to a hotel?'

'Hotel?' Chrissie stared at him. He sounded so…casual, as if he had done this dozens of times before. Which he probably had of course, she realized with a sharp stab of mingled pain and jealousy. Slowly, and with more reluctance than she cared to acknowledge, she shook her head.

'I don't think so.'

'Why not?' He cupped her chin in his hand and turned her face to his, fingers lightly caressing her throat as he did so. He could feel the heavy beat of her pulse, hear her quickened breathing of arousal. 'We both want to,' he said huskily.

'Y-yes.' She couldn't deny that. 'But…not for just one night. And that's all you want, isn't it?'

'Ah.' Trent released her and straightened up behind the steering wheel. 'How stupid of me to forget your rule – no commitment, no sex. Right?' he demanded harshly. Chrissie flinched.

'I won't be a one-night stand,' she said, but was truly appalled to discover that she was sorely tempted to be just that, if that was all he was prepared to offer.

She waited, hoping desperately for an assurance that she would be more that that. She waited in vain.

'Sorry.' He sounded faintly regretful, but certainly not devastated, and leaned across her to open the car door. He didn't even look at her as she scrambled out on to the pavement, and had driven off without a backward glance before she'd even reached her front door.

chapter eight

Celia was both surprised and disappointed to discover Trent had arrived back at the Hall before she did. He couldn't have spent any time with Chrissie at all. What a pity, and she'd put up with Judy Lawford bragging about her four grandchildren – really, one would think she had produced them herself – for no good purpose. Obviously, she might just as well have left the hotel with Trent and Chrissie after all.

She hoped they hadn't quarrelled, and went in search of Trent: he wasn't in any of the downstairs rooms, so she made her way up to his bedroom and rapped on the door. There was no reply, but she opened it anyway and heard the shower running in the adjoining bathroom.

'Is everything all right, Trent?' she called.

'Fine.'

'Can I get you any supper?'

'No. Thank you,' he added belatedly.

'I'll say goodnight, then. I suppose you'll be going back to London early in the morning?'

'Yes. I won't wake you. I'll phone you later in the week.'

'Right. I think I'll have a hot bath before bed. It's turned cold, hasn't it?'

'Certainly has in here,' Trent muttered. The shower spray was icy, deliberately so. He was shivering with cold as he towelled down, but his body still ached with unfulfilled desire for Chrissie.

He was too tense to sleep, or to concentrate on paper-work, so he sat in front of the TV set, switching through the channels hoping to find something which would hold his attention and stop him thinking about Chrissie, stop him wanting her. He had to concede that her strategy was excellent: one minute purring sex-kitten, the next coy maiden who couldn't possibly spend a night with a man. She was a challenge sure enough, he thought, his blue eyes glinting with determination. He had never been one to balk at a challenge. He would get her into bed, hopefully sooner rather than later, and it would be on his terms, not hers.

Despite an early start, Trent wasn't quite early enough to avoid becoming snarled up in London's rush hour traffic. God knows why it's called the rush hour when rushing is the last thing anyone can do, he thought, irritably drumming his fingers on the steering wheel.

He didn't reach his office until nine thirty, an almost unheard of time for him, as he was usually at his desk before any of the staff arrived. He glanced through the stack of phone messages and put those from Dan Thomson at the top of the pile.

'Coffee please, Rosa,' he requested, and went into his office, closing the door behind him. He dialled the number for Thomson and Wilson.

'Trent Fairfax for Dan Thomson,' he said briskly, then, 'Thomson? About Chrissie Brennan…'

'She's no longer employed by this firm,' Dan Thomson cut in, well pleased with himself for his handling of the awkward situation.

'I know that,' Trent snapped. 'And I know why. I've already told her she has a strong case against you if she takes you to an industrial tribunal.'

'But…' In Farminster, Dan Thomson turned grey. 'She resigned,' he protested.

'Under pressure. It was constructive dismissal, and you know it,' Trent said crisply.

'But, her honesty was in question…'

'Nonsense! You misunderstood the situation. My young brother played a silly prank on her which backfired, that's all there was to it. I suggest you apologize profusely and reinstate her immediately, unless you have any complaints about her work?'

'No, no we don't. But I've already sent her a cheque to cover the remainder of her contract.'

'Then draw up another contract. With a substantial pay increase,' Trent added for good measure. Dan Thomson was a toadying fool and deserved to pay for it. Trent had particularly wanted to appoint a local firm to handle the Tanner Lane estate, but now intended using the national chain he often dealt with. Not that he was going to tell Thomson that, at least not until Chrissie's job was secure.

'I'll do that right away,' Thomson agreed eagerly. 'Er, the Tanner Lane…'

'I'll be back in Farminster later this week,' Trent cut in. That was true; he had arranged a meeting with his architect and site manager.

He ended the call and sat back in his chair, sipping the hot strong coffee Rosa had placed before him. Dan Thomson would do as he had been told, Trent was sure of that. Therefore his debt to Chrissie was paid, or would be during the next few days. Which meant the battle of wills could begin; Chrissie's determination to keep out of his bed until he made a commitment, versus his equal determination to have her without making any promises.

He finished his coffee and set to work, pushing thoughts

of Chrissie's seduction to the back of his mind. He wouldn't contact her until Friday, he decided, the day of his scheduled meetings in Farminster. By then she would, he hoped, be worrying whether she had ruined her chances with him.

Chrissie had also spent a very restless night, tossing and turning, her body aching for his touch. Why him? she groaned. He desired her, yes, but he also despised her. He had made no secret of the latter, yet had expected her to ignore it and jump into bed with him.

Is his attitude born of his family's position in the area?' she wondered feverishly, around two in the morning when her brain had almost stopped functioning due to lack of sleep. After all, for generations *droit de seigneur* had meant that his ancestors had enjoyed the right to bed any girl from the lower classes…

She finally fell asleep, but he haunted her dreams, too: dressed in medieval armour and riding Sultan, he bore down on her. She couldn't run, could only stand, rooted to the spot and wait for him to…

She never discovered what he had been about to do, for the very modern trill of the telephone jerked her abruptly awake. For a moment she lay still, bathed in perspiration and disorientated by the dream, then she pushed back the covers and groped for the phone.

'Chrissie dear, it's Celia Fairfax. I was hoping that, as you're at a loose end, you might like to come over this morning and help me exercise the horses. And stay for lunch, of course,' she added.

It was a genuine offer: she liked Chrissie and loved having company, but she was also hoping to glean some information about what, if anything, had transpired between her and Trent the night before. Despite setting her alarm clock for five-thirty, to be sure to catch Trent before he left for London, she had overslept, and woke to discover that she had missed him.

'The horses?' Chrissie rubbed sleep from her eyes. Only someone in Celia's privileged position could describe unemployment as 'being at a loose end' she thought wryly. 'I couldn't possibly ride Sultan,' she said quickly, recalling the size of Ben's stallion. She hadn't risked even getting near him when he was safely in his stable, so she certainly wasn't going to try to ride him!

'No, of course not. You can ride Fliss and I'll take Sultan,' Celia assured her.

'You can ride Sultan?' Chrissie asked, with more doubt than tact.

'Oh yes, I'm an excellent rider, practically rode before I could walk. It's about the only thing I *do* excel at,' she sighed. 'So, will you come? I can lend you a hat if you don't have one.'

'Thank you.' Chrissie felt she ought to be out job-hunting, but Celia sounded as if she might be lonely. It must seem awfully quiet without Ben and his friends racing in and out all the time. 'Yes, I'd love to come, but be warned, I haven't ridden for ages.'

'Don't worry, you'll be fine. I'll see you later, about nine-thirty?'

'Yes,' Chrissie agreed. 'And thank you again for last night. I told Trent you were brilliant with Annabel.'

'Did you? I'm ashamed to say I quite enjoyed doing that,' Celia admitted happily. 'Bye for now, dear.'

'Bye,' Chrissie replaced the receiver, smiling. Her smile broadened as she recalled the expression on Annabel's face when Celia had called her a bitch, and felt a warm glow of affection for the older woman. She had been like a mother hen defending her chick and it was a long time since anyone had mothered Chrissie.

She didn't possess any proper riding clothes, but hoped she wouldn't seem too much of a townie in jeans, sweater and a jacket, with low-heeled boots. She drove up to Fairfax Hall shortly before nine-thirty, and after a slight hesitation used the heavy brass knocker on the carved oak front doors. She was an invited guest, after all, and invited guests used the front door, not the kitchen entrance.

'Come on in,' Celia opened the door herself and impulsively kissed Chrissie's cheek. 'I was just having coffee in the library – would you like some?'

'Yes please,' Chrissie followed her inside, and looked around with interest.

The hall was large, panelled in dark wood, yet well-lit and plushly carpeted. Huge bowls of fresh flowers, which must cost a fortune at this time of the year, were placed on numerous antique tables and the fragrance of the blooms mingled pleasantly with that of furniture polish.

The library was a comfortable, not overly-large room, with a warm, well-lived-in atmosphere. Two walls were lined from top to bottom with bookshelves, while the other two were panelled like the hall, yet, Chrissie noticed, these individual panels were exquisitely carved and decorated. She had to suppress a grin at the thought of the woodworm-infested desk nestling against such splendour. No wonder Trent had been so cross!

'Come and sit down,' Celia urged, and Chrissie followed her to where two large, squashy armchairs were ranged in front of the open fire. Celia poured coffee and handed a cup to Chrissie, pushing a tray containing cream jug and sugar bowl towards her. There was also a plate of the delicious home-made biscuits Chrissie had enjoyed the day before. 'Help yourself, dear,' Celia urged. 'I've already had four!'

'Thank you.' Chrissie didn't need telling twice.

'Molly – did you meet her? No, of course you didn't,' Celia answered her own question. 'She's our housekeeper, well she's part of the family, really, been with us for years. She's gone to the supermarket, but you'll meet her at lunch…' She chattered on, happy to have an audience but not really needing any replies, Chrissie thought, as she relaxed in the warmth from the fire.

'Did you and Trent have a nice time last night?' Celia asked suddenly. Chrissie blinked in surprise.

'Well, he only gave me a lift home,' she said.

'Oh.' Celia was disappointed. Oh well, she wasn't beaten yet, and cheered up almost at once. 'Have you had enough? Shall we go out while the sun's still shining? The forecast is for rain later,' she added, stacking cups, saucers and plates on to the tray.

'Let me carry that,' Chrissie followed her along the hall and through a door into a second, less plush hall which in turn led into the kitchen.

'Just put it down over there,' Celia nodded towards a work surface above a dishwasher. 'Oh good, you're wearing sensible boots…try this hat for size,' she produced a regulation riding hat. 'I hate the things – they mess up one's hair frightfully – but Trent insists…' She pulled on her own riding boots, put on a jacket and hat, then led the way out to the stables.

Someone had already saddled the horses in readiness for their ride and Chrissie spent a few moments making a fuss of Fliss to let the mare become accustomed to her, before she attempted to climb on her back.

Then she took a deep breath and prayed she wouldn't fall off, before putting her foot in the stirrup and swinging her leg over to the other side. Much to her amazement, she stayed on. At first it felt strange to be on a horse again and the ground seemed an awful long way down, but as Celia led the way slowly out of the courtyard to the fields beyond, she began to relax and enjoy the sensation.

'Did you have a pony when you were a child?' Celia enquired. Chrissie thought back to the council house and its small garden.

'No, I didn't learn to ride until I was seventeen,' she said, adding, 'Charles Hawksworth taught me.'

'Oh, you know the Hawksworths?'

'Yes, I met them shortly after my parents died. They were very kind to me.'

'Both your parents are dead?' Celia was shocked. 'Do you have brothers or sisters?'

'No.'

'You poor child.' She reached across and patted Chrissie's hand in sympathy. 'So you knew Charles before he went to Australia? Of course you did, silly me, you could hardly have met him since…' She stopped abruptly as it occurred to her that Chrissie might have been the girl Charles had wanted to marry. Oh dear. She hoped Trent didn't know.

'Do you feel confident enough to go a little faster?' she asked, for Sultan was getting restive at the snail's pace. Chrissie glanced down at the, hopefully soft, grass beneath the mare's hooves and nodded.

Celia urged Sultan into a trot and then a canter, with Fliss following suit without any instructions from her new rider. They climbed a gently sloping hill, with woods to one side and fields to the other, then came to a clearing at the top.

Celia reined in to admire the view and Chrissie managed to halt Fliss, although she felt it was more the mare's decision than the result of her own horsemanship. Fairfax Hall was behind them in the distance. Before them spread the Fairfax estate farms, and beyond, the outskirts of Farminster.

'When I married Philip Fairfax there was nothing to see but open countryside from up here,' Celia told her. 'Now look,' she pointed to a rash of new housing. 'Isn't it dreadful, boxy little things, such an eyesore,' she sighed.

'Trent's a builder,' Chrissie pointed out. Celia smiled slightly.

'You make it sound as if he's in charge of the cement mixer, or something,' she said lightly, then went off at a tangent as she often did. 'Although, actually, he did work on a building site, once, as a labourer,' she recalled. 'Under an assumed name, of course, because he was…undercover.'

'Why did he do that? To learn every aspect of the trade?' Chrissie guessed.

'Oh no, there was some trouble, not just the usual pilfering of tools and materials, but systematic large scale theft. He suspected the site manager, but had no proof, so he got a job on site while the man was on holiday.'

'Goodness,' Chrissie was fascinated by this new side to Trent Fairfax. 'Did he discover who was responsible?'

'Oh yes. It *was* the man he suspected; there was a court case, but it was all some years ago… Where was I? Oh yes, these horrible little houses. Trent doesn't build those. He grew up in the countryside and deplores the spread from the towns, especially as it's often not necessary. His building projects are mostly in the inner cities, clearing old warehouses and slums – what do you call it?'

'Brownfield sites…?' Chrissie supplied.

'That's it; aren't you clever?' Celia beamed at her. 'I suppose I should feel guilty, as we have so much land, but we put it to good use,' she said earnestly. 'We grow crops and raise livestock. People need food just as much as they need housing, don't they?'

'Of course,' Chrissie agreed. Celia looked down at the new housing estate once more and sighed.

'I hope they don't build any nearer to us. Does that make me a bimbo?' she asked. Chrissie stared at her, then smiled as the penny dropped.

'No, a "nimby". Not In My Back Yard,' she translated.

'Oh yes, that's right. What's a bimbo then?'

'Annabel Harrington-Smyth!' Chrissie said at once, grinning, and Celia threw back her head and laughed.

'You're quite right. Now, do you think you could manage a gallop?'

'I'll try,' Chrissie agreed bravely. 'So long as we keep on the grass,' she added prudently.

She hadn't fallen off once by the time they returned to the Hall and felt quite proud of herself. She also felt rather stiff and sore and recalled, when it was too late, how she had suffered agonies the day after her first long ride with Charles. She was going to regret this tomorrow!

Back at the house, she met Molly, a pleasant woman of around Celia's age who had prepared lunch while they were out. The three of them ate together in a small break-fast room adjacent to the kitchen.

'I hope you don't mind eating in here, we only use the dining room for formal occasions,' Celia explained.

'Not at all,' Chrissie assured her. She was ravenous after the fresh air and exercise and the food was delicious:

home-made steak and kidney pie followed by blackberry and apple crumble with cream.

'This is wonderful – how do you manage to stay so slim?' she asked Celia, who smiled, pleased by the compliment.

'Worrying about my boys, I expect,' she said lightly, but probably truthfully, Chrissie thought. She must have worried constantly about Ben's reckless driving and heavy drinking. And Trent's broken marriage...

Chrissie desperately wanted to ask about that, but resisted the urge to pry. She was sure Trent would hate it if he knew she'd been probing, and Celia might resent being asked about such a personal family matter. But, most of all, she stayed silent because she didn't want to risk hearing how much Trent had loved his wife. And obviously still did.

After their meal, Chrissie helped Molly clear away and load the dishwasher while Celia made coffee.

'Would you like me to drive you to the hospital to visit Ben?' Chrissie asked Celia. Celia hesitated: she was sure Trent would prefer it if Chrissie didn't go near Ben, but how to achieve that without hurting the poor girl? If she weren't careful, she would give the impression that she disapproved of the relationship. Which she did, of course, but only because she believed Chrissie would be wonderful for Trent, not because she thought she would be bad for Ben, or that she was a fortune hunter.

Celia wasn't very clear about the circumstances surrounding the disappearance of the emerald, but she somehow felt sure that Chrissie was not interested in either the ring or Ben. But she was equally sure that Trent would be happier if Chrissie didn't spend time with Ben. And Trent's happiness – or, rather, the present lack of it –

was what concerned her most.

'Thank you for the offer,' she said warmly, 'but Molly can take me. I think you had better spend the afternoon having a long soak in a hot bath,' having noticed Chrissie rubbing her posterior and aching thighs.

'You're probably right,' Chrissie agreed. 'Will you tell him I'll call in tonight instead?' Damn, thought Celia, biting her lip in annoyance.

'Of course I will, dear,' she smiled brightly.

While Chrissie was running her bath, she heard a knock on her front door and, groaning slightly, went back down the stairs she had only just dragged herself up. It was her next door neighbour, Mrs Campbell, a nice enough elderly lady but lonely and inclined to chat.

'I'm running a bath,' Chrissie got in quickly, then her eyes widened at the sight of the bouquet of flowers Mrs Campbell was holding.

'You were out when the delivery man came, so I said I'd make sure you got them,' she beamed. 'I put them in water so they'd keep fresh.'

'That was kind of you, thank you,' Chrissie smiled as she took the bouquet. Not red roses, so hopefully not from Ben. These were like a breath of fresh air, a colourful promise of Spring – daffodils, narcissi, iris and tulips.

She searched for a card, her heart thudding painfully, and her fingers shook as she ripped open the small envelope. They had to be from Trent…

They were from Dan Thomson, and her disappointment was shattering.

'They're not from your young man, then?' Mrs Campbell could see she was less than pleased.

'No,' Chrissie forced a smile. 'But thank you for taking

them in. I really must go; I've left the bath taps running…'

'Oh, of course. Goodbye, Chrissie.'

'Bye.' Chrissie closed the door, dumped the flowers unceremoniously on to the floor and climbed back upstairs, reading the card as she went.

Many apologies for the misunderstanding. Please
give me a call to arrange a meeting. Regards,
Dan Thomson.

Huh! 'Misunderstanding…? Yeah, right,' she muttered, unimpressed.

She turned off the taps, undressed, and lowered herself gingerly into the almost scalding water, sighing blissfully as she stretched out her limbs and felt the heat easing the ache in her sore muscles.

Trent had moved fast, she thought, and must have scared Dan Thomson witless for him to have got the flowers to her so quickly. She just wished they were from Trent, to show her he wasn't angry about her refusal to spend the night with him. She didn't suppose he was accustomed to being told 'no' – something he had in common with Ben!

As for Dan Thomson…a rather nice cheque had arrived in the post that morning, which probably accounted for her lack of urgency on that score. In fact, she wasn't at all sure she wanted to return to the estate agency, particularly after the way in which she had left. Thomson had shown a lack of loyalty to a member of staff which didn't bode well for a future working relationship. Now, with three months' salary in the bank, she had a breathing space, and decided it would be folly not at least to have a look at what else was on offer, before she went meekly back to Thomson and Wilson.

She stayed in the bath for an hour, replenishing the hot

water several times, and reading a novel she'd received as a Christmas gift but not had time to read. What a way to spend a weekday afternoon! She could get used to such decadence, she thought happily, and only hauled herself out when the phone began to ring.

She hastily wrapped a bath towel around her and padded to her bedroom, snatching up the phone. Once again she felt a searing disappointment: the caller wasn't Trent, it was Sally.

'What's going on?' Sally demanded, without preamble. 'I've just seen the evening paper. There's a front page picture of you and Celia Fairfax looking very chummy at the Park Hotel! She *is* Ben's mother, I take it?'

'Yes.'

'I don't get it. Last week, Trent Fairfax wanted to put you in gaol and now it looks as if the family's adopted you!' she exclaimed. Chrissie grinned.

'It was a PR exercise in damage limitation,' she told her.

'Come again?'

'Trent found the ring, so he and his mother thought they owed it to me to try and stop the rumours spreading any further,' she explained. 'It was Celia's idea to go to the fashion show and make sure we had our picture taken together.'

'Ooh, 'Celia' is it?' Sally laughed. 'Very pally.'

'She's sweet,' Chrissie protested.

'OK, I was only kidding; I'm glad Trent Fairfax is off your back.' She lowered her voice as if afraid of being overheard. 'I heard Dan Thomson tearing a strip off Reg Ford this morning; it was something about you and Trent Fairfax, so I guess we know who dropped you in it with the boss.'

'Reg, you mean?'

'It sounded like it.'

'Dan sent me some flowers,' Chrissie told her. 'I think he was acting under orders from Trent.'

'Oh great! So you're coming back?' Sally asked eagerly. 'It's no fun without you.'

'I'm not sure if I will come back, Sal,' Chrissie said slowly. 'Are you rushed off your feet?'

'Not really. The part-timers are working extra hours, for now anyway. I suppose they'll advertise for someone else if you decide not to come back.'

'Mmm.' Chrissie hadn't considered that. Of course they would want a replacement; she couldn't dither about for very long. Apart from any other consideration, it wasn't fair to Sally, for she would bear the brunt of Chrissie's absence. Perhaps she would call Dan Thomson after all, and keep her options open, for a few days at least. If there was nothing of interest on offer at the Job Centre, maybe she would go back...*if* Dan Thomson was sufficiently apologetic.

'Are you coming to aerobics class tonight?' Sally asked next. Chrissie winced at the mere thought of more exercise.

'No, I'm going to see Ben,' she said. 'I'll call you tomorrow.'

'OK. Can I tell Mr Thomson you're seriously considering coming back?'

'Yes, but stress how upset I am by what happened and how I need a few days holiday to recover from the trauma,' Chrissie said, giggling.

'Don't talk to me about stress! I'll be the one needing a holiday if these part-timers don't get their act together,' Sally grumbled. 'I'd better go; there are calls waiting. Bye.'

Chrissie replaced the receiver and went to get dressed.

The hot soak had greatly helped her muscles so she was moving easily as she got into the Mini and set out for the hospital. It was in stark contrast to her ancient-crone-impersonation after arriving home from Fairfax Hall, stiff and weary, just a few hours earlier.

She remembered Trent telling her how depressed Ben had been the night before, and hoped his spirits had lifted. He seemed pleased to see her, giving a broad grin when she entered his room.

'It's great to see you: I thought you'd gone off me,' he grumbled, but good-naturedly.

'Didn't Trent tell you why I didn't come last night?' she asked, pulling up a chair.

'Yeah, some charity bash with Ma,' he nodded.

'And you know he found the ring?'

'Yes. He said he's putting it back in the bank,' he scowled slightly.

'That's the best place for it, Ben,' Chrissie said gently. 'Can't we forget all that nonsense and just be friends?'

'I've got all the friends I need.' His scowl deepened.

'Aren't you lucky?' Chrissie said brightly, ignoring his petulance.

'I know what's been going on,' Ben said suddenly.

'What do you mean?' Chrissie asked. She was afraid she looked guilty, which was ridiculous because she had nothing to feel guilty about.

'You and Trent, the devious bastard. I suppose he told you about Annabel staying the night at my place after the party, and then pounced when you became upset…'

'Hey, just hold on a second. Did I hear right? You and Annabel? You spent the night with her…the night you proposed to me?' Chrissie demanded incredulously. She felt as if a huge weight was being lifted from her shoulders.

'Trent didn't tell you?' Ben sighed, slowly realizing he had just shot himself in the foot.

'No, but you have!' she pointed out. 'So let's not have any more stupid talk about engagements, OK?' she asked. Ben ignored that.

'Trent's only trying to break us up, you do realize that? He doesn't even like you, so I hope you're not taking him seriously,' he warned.

'I don't know what you're talking about?' she muttered.

'Yes, you do. Annabel saw him kissing you,' Ben told her flatly.

'She did? When?' Chrissie asked, unthinkingly.

'When?' Ben repeated. 'How many times has he kissed you?' he demanded furiously.

'Um, not many,' she mumbled.

'Oh, Chrissie…!' Ben reached over and took hold of her hand. 'You're not falling in love with him, are you?' he asked gently, all anger forgotten.

Chrissie looked at him, saw the sympathy in the blue eyes so like his brother's, and had to blink back tears.

'I hope not.' She tried to smile.

'So do I. For your sake.' He squeezed her hand comfortingly. 'You'd have much more fun with me!'

'You and Annabel, presumably?' Chrissie asked dryly. He grinned.

'You know what they say – the more, the merrier!'

'You're incorrigible.' She leaned over to kiss his cheek. Ben turned his face quickly and held the back of her neck so that she kissed him on the mouth instead. Which was what Annabel saw when she strolled in.

'Oh. Hello, Kirsty,' she said coldly. Chrissie was

tempted to respond in similar fashion, but found she simply couldn't be bothered. Instead, she picked up her bag and got to her feet.

'Hello, Annabel. It's OK, he's all yours,' she said graciously, then turned back to Ben. 'By the way, that "devious bastard" is so concerned about you, that he's arranging for you to have private nursing at home as soon as your doctor says you can leave here. Goodbye.'

She walked serenely out of the room, leaving behind a shamefaced Ben and a furious Annabel. Taking Ben away from Chrissie was one thing, having him handed over was quite another! Still, a slight smile curved her thin lips, if the silly chit was setting her cap at Trent Fairfax, she'd get her come-uppance soon enough.

chapter nine

Chrissie had intended going to the Job Centre first thing on Wednesday morning, but a letter in the post pushed all other thoughts from her mind.

She read it quickly, then again more slowly, and for a third time as she switched on the kettle to make coffee. The letter was from a local firm of solicitors who, acting on behalf of an unnamed client, were offering to buy her cottage. It was a reasonable price, too, she noted absently. Property values had risen since she had purchased her home and, after repaying her mortgage, she would have quite a lot of money left. *If* she sold.

The burning question though, was who exactly the mystery client was? She knew there was no point in asking, for they wouldn't divulge his identity. She didn't want to face up to it, but the obvious answer was Trent Fairfax. He knew she had no job and, if she sold her house, there would be nothing to keep her in Farminster...

Was he making doubly sure she didn't drift back into a relationship with Ben? Perhaps he was afraid that Ben, bored in his long convalescence, would have nothing better to do than pursue her if she was still living locally? She felt sure Trent Fairfax was always very thorough, but, actually to buy her out? That was a bit extreme, even for someone with his wealth. Yet, of course, he could simply resell it, she realized, and he might even make a profit!

The suspicion that he was behind the offer settled over

her like a black cloud, and since she was already depressed, she glumly decided she might as well make one of her trips to the cemetery, to check on her parents' grave. She didn't go often, for she had never had any sense of them being there in any way. She kept the double grave tidy, but derived no comfort from going there.

As she left the house, she saw Mrs Campbell beckoning to her from next door, but pretending not to see her, got quickly into her car and sped away. She parked near the cemetery and walked inside; there was a funeral taking place and she took a detour to avoid the mourners. She passed an old lady busily arranging flowers and chatting happily to her late husband, telling him all the latest family news and local gossip.

Chrissie smiled a little wistfully, wishing she could chat away to her parents in the same way and be sure they could hear her and understand. Maybe even offer advice, for she certainly felt the need of loving guidance. Was it time for her to leave Farminster? Perhaps all the recent events were omens she shouldn't ignore. After her parents had died, she had wanted, needed, to stay in the familiar surroundings of her childhood, but she no longer felt that way.

She knelt down beside the grave and tidied the covering gravel, still fairly neat after the winter with no weeds pushing through. The bulbs she had planted around the border last Autumn were doing well; snowdrops and crocuses already blooming and the hyacinths were showing promise of blue and pink flowers to come.

She wiped down the matching headstones with a damp cloth, then sat back on her heels.

'I wish you could help me,' she whispered, feeling selfconscious about talking out loud, but it obviously helped the old lady she had seen, and it couldn't do any harm.

She closed her eyes and concentrated hard, trying to figure out what their advice would have been. She already knew, though: they would have told her what she didn't want to hear, namely that she should stay away from Trent Fairfax; that men like him used girls from the lower orders for their pleasure but only married those from their own class. Had Francesca been of the gentry? she wondered. If so, it hadn't done either her or Trent much good...

Why am I even thinking about marriage? He only wanted a one-night stand and had never pretended otherwise. Berating herself for her stupidity, she stood up, dusted off her jeans and walked back the way she had come.

The old lady was still chatting away to her captive audience. She saw Chrissie watching but wasn't a bit perturbed at being caught talking to a headstone. She smiled, wished her 'good morning' and continued with her one-sided conversation. Chrissie returned the smile and the greeting, and went back to her car.

Mrs Campbell was apparently watching out for her, and waved frenziedly from her front porch. Chrissie sighed; it was obviously going to be her day for dealing with batty old ladies.

'Hello, Mrs Campbell. Do you need me to do some shopping for you?'

'No, thank you, Chrissie. I wanted a word – did you receive an offer for your house in this morning's post?'

'Yes, I did,' Chrissie walked slowly towards her. 'You, too?'

'Yes. And next door; I've already checked. I don't know about Mr Gregson at Number Eight – he had already left for work when I knocked, but I peered through the letter box and I'm fairly sure he's got a letter, too. The typing on the envelope is the same as mine,' she said. Miss Marple lives, Chrissie thought absently, her mind buzzing with conflicting thoughts. Surely this was overkill, even for Trent Fairfax?

'It'll be the land they're after,' Mrs Campbell was way ahead of her.

'Sorry?'

'The land. We've all got long back gardens and there's that orchard at the bottom. It'll be a builder, mark my words. I bet he's already got his hands on the orchard, and wants a bit extra. The way they cram them on to tiny plots these days, well, there must be room for thirty houses or more. Don't you agree?'

'Well…'

'Hadn't you heard about it before today? You do work in an estate agency, don't you?' Mrs Campbell eyed her doubtfully. Chrissie was still thinking about Trent Fairfax.

'Yes, I mean, no, I hadn't heard anything about it. But you're probably right,' she agreed. 'Are you thinking of selling?'

'I think I might. I've lived here for thirty years, but the garden is too big and the stairs are becoming too difficult for me. I was going to have one of those stair-lifts installed, but now I think I'd prefer a nice new bungalow. They're offering a lot of money for these cottages, aren't they?' she added brightly.

'Compared to what you paid thirty years ago, I'm sure it does seem a lot,' Chrissie said carefully, 'but it certainly isn't overly generous. If I were you, I'd look at prices of bungalows before making a decision.'

'Oh yes, I will,' Mrs Campbell nodded.

'I can get you some brochures later – I have to go back into town,' Chrissie offered.

'Thank you, that would be a great help,' Mrs Campbell beamed. 'Now, I think we should have a meeting; all the neighbours, I mean. I asked Jan and Mike and they said they'd come, and I can put a note through Mr Gregson's letter box. How about you? Will seven o clock tonight suit you?'

'Yes, all right,' Chrissie agreed: it couldn't hurt to hear what the others intended doing. 'I'll see you later.'

The news that her neighbours had received similar offers didn't help much in trying to figure out whether Trent Fairfax was the unnamed client. After all, he was a builder and would have instinctively spotted the potential in the under-developed site so close to the town centre. Perhaps he had seized the chance of making a profit out of getting rid of her?

She picked up the solicitor's letter and checked the date: of course, when the offer had been made, Trent had still believed her responsible for the loss of the ring. She wondered whether he would tell her the truth if she asked him outright if he was behind the offer to buy her house, but decided against phoning him. The decision to sell or not should be based on the merits of the offer, and nothing else, she told herself firmly.

Her trip to the Job Centre proved disappointing; there was nothing that caught her interest. Perhaps she should stop messing about and call Dan Thomson? After all, she had enjoyed working at Thomson and Wilson. Unless she should take the lack of suitable jobs as another sign that it was time for her to move away?

She did some shopping for herself, then began the rounds of the estate agents to collect a selection of brochures for Mrs Campbell. Dan Thomson was gazing out of his office window when he spotted Chrissie entering a rival's showroom opposite, and he began to sweat. Trent Fairfax would never sign the contract if Chrissie Brennan went to work elsewhere! He was sweating even more by the time he had pounded down the stairs, out of the office and chased Chrissie along the street.

'Chrissie! Miss Brennan!' he gasped. Chrissie turned at the sound of her name, saw who wanted her attention and tried her best to look traumatised by the ordeal he had subjected her to. She even managed to cringe away slightly when he approached, as if frightened of what he might do.

'Chrissie, my dear girl,' he smiled ingratiatingly. 'I've been hoping you would call me, but how about lunch? We can have a chat and discuss a new contract of employment.'

'The last one wasn't worth the paper it was written on,' Chrissie retorted, forgetting she was supposed to be cowed. 'You had no reason to sack me.'

'You resigned, you...'

'You accused me of dishonesty – I had no choice but to resign!' she interrupted hotly.

'I was wrong,' he admitted, with what she guessed was meant to be a winning smile. 'I would very much like you to come back. You're a great asset to the firm, your lovely face is good for business...'

'That remark constitutes sexual harassment,' Chrissie told him; she was beginning to enjoy herself. Dan Thomson took out his handkerchief and mopped his brow.

'You could do more work on the estate agency side and

less on reception,' he said, knowing that would tempt her. 'And you'd have a rise in salary, of course.'

'I'm not sure,' she wavered.

'Let me buy you lunch,' he offered again, and Chrissie knew, from his rather smug smile, that he thought he had won.

'Sorry, not today,' she declined coolly. 'But I'll think about coming back to work and let you know my decision as soon as possible.' After all, it wasn't fair to the other staff, particularly Sally, to procrastinate for too long.

'It would be a long-term contract this time,' he added icing to the cake. Chrissie refused to be impressed.

'I'm not sure I'd be interested in working for you long-term. In fact, I might be leaving Farminster soon.' She turned to walk away. Then she remembered that she had been brought up to have good manners even though he patently hadn't, and turned back. 'Thank you for the flowers,' she said politely.

'My pleasure,' he stared after her. Leaving Farminster? He wished he knew whether that was good news for him, or bad.

Chrissie joined her neighbours at seven that evening, all of them crowding into Mrs Campbell's living room. Mrs Campbell had already carefully studied the brochures Chrissie had dropped off earlier, and was quite excited at the prospect of a move to a brand new retirement bungalow nearby. She had been shocked by the price, though, and realized that she would have to pay as much as she had been offered for her cottage.

Jan and Mike, a couple in their early thirties who lived at Number Six, were also keen to take up the offer. They planned to start a family soon and had already been considering a move to a larger property.

'It's a bit sooner than we'd thought, but at least this way we'll save on estate agency fees trying to sell ours,' Jan said, adding hastily, 'No offence, Chrissie.'

'None taken,' she smiled, and turned to Bill Gregson, the bachelor at Number Eight. 'How about you?'

'Well, if the rest of you are selling, I guess I will, too,' he said. 'I certainly don't want to live on the edge of a new housing estate. But are you sure that is what's being planned?' He looked at Chrissie, who shrugged.

'I think it must be,' she said. 'Especially if they've already got hold of the orchard. Does anyone know who owns that?' she asked. Everyone shook their heads.

'I can probably find out,' offered Jan, who worked in the council offices.

'What about the price?' Mike put in, again looking to Chrissie for guidance. She wondered vaguely how they would all react if they knew Thomson and Wilson had sacked her, wondered too how they would feel if they discovered it was Trent Fairfax who was disrupting their lives because of his vendetta against her. Still, no one's forcing anyone to go, she consoled herself.

'It's reasonable, no more than that,' she told him.

'But they obviously want us out – will they go higher?' he persisted.

'Probably,' she nodded.

'Really?' Mrs Campbell perked up. 'Another couple of thousand would be lovely,' she sighed.

'I'd want more than that,' Bill Gregson interjected. 'And, since they want us to go, they should pay our solicitor's fees,' he added firmly.

'Do you expect them to move your furniture, as well?' Mike asked sarcastically. 'If we ask for too much, they could back out and make a similar offer elsewhere,' he pointed out. 'I don't think we should be too greedy.'

'That's easy for you to say – you were already planning a move,' Bill shot back. They continued bickering about how much extra they could expect, and Chrissie grew restive.

'I'll go along with whatever the rest of you decide,' she said, getting to her feet. 'But I have to go now.'

'Goodbye, Chrissie, and thank you so much for bringing me those brochures,' Mrs Campbell opened the door for her.

'You're welcome. Goodnight, everybody,' she gave a general wave to the others and hopped across the low fence to her own front garden.

She heard her phone ringing as she unlocked the door, and rushed to answer it. Her heart leaped with joy when she heard Trent's voice. Careful, she warned herself; he's probably only calling to try to discover your reaction to the sale offer.

'What's this I hear about you leaving Farminster?' he demanded, without preamble.

'How do you know I might be leaving?' she asked suspiciously.

'Dan Thomson told me. He's running scared about not being appointed sole agent for the Tanner Lane estate. I may have given him the impression he would only get the contract if you returned to work for him,' he said smoothly, but with an underlying note of satisfaction.

'*May* have given the impression…?' Chrissie repeated. Suddenly, she felt she was bursting with happiness. If Trent had gone to all that trouble to have her reinstated, it didn't make any sense at all for him to be going to a lot of expense to get her out of her house.

'OK, I definitely gave that impression!' he admitted cheerfully. 'So why did you tell him you might be leaving town? Were you serious, or were you just hoping to get a bigger pay rise?'

'No, I really am thinking about going,' she told him.

'Why? You're not running away from the gossip, are you?' he asked, but quite gently.

'Not at all. I'm twenty-two and I've lived here all my life. I've only been abroad a couple of times, on package holidays to Spain. Now I've had an offer for my house,' she continued, hoping her voice didn't betray her suspicion that he already knew all about it. 'After I pay off my mortgage, I'll have quite a bit left over. It seems a good opportunity to do some travelling.'

'I see.' His voice was neutral, betraying nothing. Chrissie tried to get a reaction.

'I thought you'd be pleased,' she taunted. 'After all, there would be no danger of Ben following me, not in his present condition.'

Trent ignored that. 'What did you mean, about an offer for your house?'

'I had a letter from a solicitor this morning wanting to know if I would be prepared to sell. So did my neighbours,' she added, but purposely made no mention of the larger tract of land in the form of the orchard. Let him think they hadn't cottoned on to the possibility of that being part of the purchase. 'We assume the offer's from a local, small builder,' she went on, trying to picture the expression on his face at being described – if it really was him – as a 'small' builder.

'Sounds feasible. I bet he's pitched in a low bid, though. Present a united front with your neighbours and hold out for more,' he advised. Chrissie almost dropped the receiver. What was this – double bluff? Or was he really not the 'client' who had made the offer?

'Mmm, that's what we thought we'd do. We all got together earlier this evening,' she told him.

'Good. Let me know if I can do anything to help,' he said briskly. 'I talked to Ma earlier – she was telling me how much she enjoyed your company yesterday.'

'Was she?' Chrissie was pleased. 'I enjoyed myself, too,' she told him.

'Maybe you could go and visit her again soon? I think she gets a bit lonely – all her cronies seem obsessed with playing bridge or golf, neither of which Ma's any good at.'

'Perhaps I could take her to an antiques auction,' Chrissie teased, and he groaned.

'No, please, anything but that! A shopping trip to London would be preferable, although my mother can clean out Harrods faster than a swarm of locusts can strip a cornfield, so I don't suggest that lightly.'

'OK, not antiques,' Chrissie agreed, before adding, 'I went to see Ben last night.'

'Oh?' He sounded noncommittal.

'We've decided to be friends, nothing more,' she told him. He said nothing, but she guessed he must be pleased. 'But there is one thing I don't understand.' She hesitated for a second. 'You were so anti-Ben and me, so why didn't you tell me that he spent the night of our so-called engagement with Annabel?'

'Several reasons,' he said slowly. 'For one, I balked at telling tales while Ben was in hospital and had amnesia about the whole thing – although I suspect his loss of memory is somewhat selective,' he added dryly. 'Secondly, I wanted you to end the relationship because you knew it was wrong for you both, not because your pride was hurt. And thirdly…' She could almost hear the smile in his voice. 'Forget thirdly; I'd have told you eventually, if I'd had to.'

'I rather think Annabel would have beaten you to it,' Chrissie said wryly. 'In fact, you might have to get that horrible ring back from the bank again, quite soon!'

'Don't say that; I'll have nightmares,' he groaned, before adding quickly, 'Hold on a sec, will you?' She heard the murmur of voices in the background and then another phone ringing nearby. 'Sorry about that, Chrissie.'

'Are you at your office?' she checked her watch; it was eight-thirty.

'Yes, I have a late meeting. In fact, I have to go now. But listen, I'll be back in Farminster on Friday for a meeting with the architect and site manager of the Tanner Lane project. Can I take you out to dinner afterwards?' he asked, rather casually, as if the invitation were an after-thought.

Chrissie was dumbstruck, and knew she ought to decline. But she wanted to go! 'Why? As another exercise in damage limitation…?' she strove to speak lightly.

'No, merely an apology for all the trouble my brother and I have caused you recently,' he said smoothly. Adding silently, *And to seduce you, my sweet*!

'All right, I'll come,' Chrissie said shyly. Common sense told her that she was in danger of falling for him in a big way, but she simply didn't care. She wanted to go out to dinner with him; end of debate.

'Good,' he sounded genuinely pleased, she thought. 'I'll pick you up at seven. Bye for now,' he added, and broke the connection before she could have second thoughts.

He had already decided where to take her: to the White Hart at Cloverhill, a few miles from Farminster. It had an excellent, intimate restaurant. It was also a hotel which boasted four-poster beds in every luxurious suite.

Chrissie spent the next forty-six-and-a-half hours in a high state of mingled nervousness and excitement. First she tried on every dress in her wardrobe, discarded each one as not being sophisticated enough for dinner with Trent Fairfax, and then decided to hit the shops.

She persuaded herself she could afford something new; either she would be returning to a better paid position at Thomson and Wilson, or she would be loaded after selling her cottage. Where she would actually live in that event was a question she dismissed as being irrelevant.

She found an elegant black dress in a boutique she usually avoided as being too expensive unless they had a sale on. It was close-fitting, knee-length, with spaghetti straps, and she didn't need the gushing salesgirl to tell her that it looked terrific, and very sexy.

She already owned a pair of spike-heeled black strap shoes and a suitable bag, but bought a pair of very expensive, very sheer black tights. In fact, they were so flimsy she was afraid she would poke her finger through them while putting them on, so she bought a second pair as insurance.

Back home, she experimented with her hair. Usually she either left it swinging loose to her shoulders, or tied it back in a ponytail. Neither style seemed very chic...

She tried piling it on top of her head, which made her neck seem extra long and slender, but she needed so many hair pins to make it secure that she felt like a porcupine. And she'd have his eye out if he got close... The thought of Trent getting close enough to be damaged by her hair-pins sent her off into a daydream which was broken only by the sound of repeated knocking on her door.

'Coming!' she called out, hastily dragging the pins from her hair and grimacing at herself in the mirror for her fantasies. She would look an utter fool if his meeting over-ran and he took her to the local Pizza Hut! After all, he was only taking her out because he felt bad about his suspicions over the ring and the subsequent furore over her job, she reminded herself, as she ran downstairs to open the door, only to wish she hadn't bothered when she discovered her visitor was a double-glazing salesman.

She kept on telling herself throughout Friday that she was setting herself up for heartbreak if she read anything other than an apology in his invitation, but it didn't dampen her excitement.

She was ready far too early, her hair washed, conditioned and blow-dried so that it hung in a shining, glossy bob to her shoulders. Her make-up was as perfectly applied as possible, her nails manicured and polished.

She saw the Mercedes pulling into the kerb and snatched up her bag and her black velvet jacket. She dashed down the stairs, only to stop and freeze halfway down as if taking part in a game of Grandmother's Foot-steps. *Wait*...wait until he rings the doorbell, she commanded herself. When he did, she forced herself to count slowly to ten and only then did she descend the second half of the steps and open the door.

'Hi,' Trent smiled warmly, making no attempt to hide his appreciation of her face and figure. Chrissie thought he looked wonderful, in a charcoal grey suit, white shirt and discreetly patterned silk tie.

'Hello,' she said, feeling suddenly shy and awkward.

'You look stunning,' he told her. 'It's a pity to cover up that dress, but it has turned rather cold; you'll need your jacket.' He took it from her and placed it over her shoulders, deliberately letting his fingers caress her neck as he lifted her hair free of the jacket. Chrissie shivered slightly, and not from the cool evening air, either; they were both aware of that.

'Th-thank you,' she stammered, clutching the jacket to her as she struggled to lock the door.

'Let me help.' Trent placed his large hand over her smaller one and held it for a long moment, feeling the rapid beat of her pulse beneath his fingers, then he turned the key, removed it from the lock and handed it to her.

'Thank you,' she said again.

Trent steered her down the path, one hand lightly on the small of her back, and helped her into the car. As he walked round to the driver's side he noticed her shrug off the jacket, and he smiled slightly. The Mercedes had a very efficient heating system.

'Where are we going?' Chrissie asked.

'The White Hart at Cloverhill; the food's very good there,' he said casually, wondering whether she knew that it was a hotel as well as a restaurant. She did, but the significance passed over her head.

'Yes, a friend of mine held her wedding reception there last year,' she commented. 'How did your meeting go today?'

'Fine, I think we ironed out all the problems. How about you? Have you decided whether to sell your cottage?'

'Not definitely. But we – my neighbours and I – are going to send a letter signed by us all, asking for a better price,' she said, cringing a little at how mercenary it sounded. He already thought she was a money-grabber and now she'd just confirmed it. Though apparently not, she realized gladly, when he nodded approvingly – perhaps he expected everyone to look out for their own best interests in business dealings.

'How much are you asking for?' he asked idly.

When she told him, he surprised her by suggesting that she and her neighbours should ask for a much higher figure.

'Really? Thanks for the advice.'

'No thanks are necessary – I'm merely bumping up a rival company's costs!' he said, with a broad grin. Chrissie smiled back, suddenly positive he wasn't behind the offer after all, and feeling blissfully happy that he hadn't wanted her to leave Farminster.

The White Hart was set in extensive grounds; the driveway, gardens and old, white-washed timbered building were decorated with strings of tiny fairy-lights, and the effect was to offer a welcome before guests had even arrived.

Inside, on the ground floor there was a bar and a comfortable coffee lounge as well as the dining room. Trent opened his mouth to suggest a drink before going in to eat, when he spotted James Hawksworth sitting at the bar.

Hell! That was all he needed! For all he knew, James still bore Chrissie a grudge for what had happened between her and his son, Charles, years before. After all, the man had felt it necessary to send his only child halfway around the world to get him away from Chrissie; that was hardly the kind of thing one forgave and forgot very easily. If he saw her and was rude, or even abusive, Trent's carefully planned evening would be ruined.

chapter ten

'Do you mind if we go straight in to dinner?' he asked quickly, steering Chrissie away from the bar and towards the dining room. 'I only had time to grab a sandwich at lunch and I'm ravenous. We can order drinks at the table.'

'That's fine by me,' she agreed readily; she'd been too nervous to eat much at lunchtime.

Trent wished, too late, that he had requested one of the secluded alcove tables, where James Hawksworth would be unlikely to see them, even if he did come in for a meal. However, when he had booked, he had decided that Chrissie might become nervous in such an obviously intimate setting and had instead opted for a table near the windows overlooking the gardens. The view was not as pretty as it would be in a few months' time, but was still attractive, with a fountain and statuary dotted along the gravelled drive.

Chrissie's butterflies had subsided a little and she studied the menu with interest, for the delicious aromas wafting from the kitchen were making her feel hungry.

'Have you decided what you'd like?' Trent asked, beckoning to the waiter.

'Yes. I'd like the melon and raspberry starter and then the lamb, please,' she smiled at the waiter. He returned the smile and removed the menu.

'And for you, sir?'

'I'll have the lobster bisque and, yes, the lamb to follow for me, as well,' he decided. 'What about wine, Chrissie?'

he looked across at her enquiringly. 'Do you have any particular preference?'

'No, I usually drink supermarket plonk,' she admitted cheerfully, and could swear she saw the waiter wince. Trent did, too, and he was hiding a smile as he ordered two bottles of wine, the vintage and price of which seemed to mollify the waiter somewhat.

Trent chatted amiably throughout the meal, taking pains to put her at her ease whilst unobtrusively topping up her wine glass at regular intervals.

'I'm drinking more than my fair share,' she said at one point. 'Oh, but you're driving, aren't you?' she added guilelessly. Not if I can help it, my sweet, Trent thought, his mind already on the delights awaiting in the four-poster bed upstairs.

He could see that Chrissie was relaxing more with each passing minute. Her cheeks were slightly flushed and her pansy violet eyes sparkled – and not only from the effects of the wine she had consumed. She was very aware of him, he could tell.

He had made no overt moves to touch her, not even a light touch to her hand, but he knew she noticed every time he allowed his appreciative gaze to linger slightly too long on her face or figure. When she leaned back in her chair a little to allow the waiter to place her pudding before her, the bodice of her dress pulled tight across her breasts. Trent looked directly at the soft firm curves and saw her nipples harden beneath his admiring glance. Good.

'We'll have coffee and brandy in the lounge,' he told the waiter, adding to Chrissie, 'we'll be more comfortable in there.'

'All right,' she smiled and began tucking into her

Pavlova. Trent toyed with a piece of stilton on his plate, anxious now to be out of the public eye. Everything was going according to plan, he thought, smugly – and, had he but realized, prematurely.

'Hello, Trent! I thought it was you!' James Hawksworth boomed, slapping Trent heartily on the shoulder. Hell's teeth! Trent thought grimly, getting quickly to his feet, as if he could shield Chrissie. Too late.

'And Chrissie! Hello, my dear,' James stooped and kissed her cheek while Trent looked on in amazement. This was the same man who had sent his son to Australia because he disapproved of his relationship with Chrissie? A dreadful suspicion that James had wanted Chrissie for himself insinuated itself into Trent's mind and he considered the older man carefully. He would have been in his late forties at the time, and was still lean and trim with a full head of slightly greying hair.

'Hello, Mr Hawksworth,' Chrissie greeted him with a smile and no hint of apprehension. Mr Hawksworth, not James, Trent noted with relief.

'What are you doing here?' Trent asked, rather too abruptly, but James seemed not to notice his tone.

'I had to get out of the house. Sara's got the decorators in and the smell of paint is driving me to drink,' he explained. 'If I have to look at one more colour chart or samples of wallpaper, I shall probably commit murder,' he added. 'I'm glad I've bumped into you, Chrissie,' he continued. 'Charles is coming home and we're throwing a party for him. You will come, won't you?'

'I'd love to,' she smiled happily, unaware of Trent grinding his teeth in annoyance. 'Is he coming home for good, or just a visit?'

'Oh, just a visit,' James said, which mollified Trent

somewhat. 'He loves the life out there, he thinks of it as "home" these days,' he added.

'And his visit is the reason for Mrs Hawksworth's redecorating?' Chrissie could just imagine the state Sara Hawksworth was in at the prospect of Charles coming him.

'Yes. As if Charles will even notice!' he said ruefully. He glanced at Trent, who still stood to one side as if made of stone.

Trent couldn't believe that he was hearing correctly. Charles Hawksworth was returning to England – and James obviously had no objection to him meeting up with Chrissie? *He might not, but I bloody do!* Trent told himself grimly.

'You're invited, too, Trent,' James said, not sure if he and Chrissie were what his wife called 'an item'. He had a vague idea that she'd told him Chrissie was seeing Ben Fairfax, not Trent, but he could have got it wrong. His wife's chatter went in one ear and out the other – it was the only way he could keep a hold on his sanity.

'What?' Trent stared. 'Yes…er…thank you, I'll look forward to it,' he added quickly, remembering his manners.

'Celia, too. And Ben if he's well enough. Nasty accident, so I hear?'

'Yes, it was, but he's on the mend,' Trent told him.

'That's good. Well, I'll leave you to enjoy your meal,' James nodded jovially and headed back towards the bar.

Trent watched him go, his brain buzzing with unanswered questions. He sat down again and made a pretence of eating while Chrissie polished off her Pavlova. She was a little subdued, casting anxious glances surreptitiously at Trent's unreadable expression. She wasn't sure how he was reacting to news of Charles's homecoming.

'Ready for coffee?' he asked, his voice betraying nothing of what he might be feeling. 'How about a liqueur?'

'No, thank you,' she declined; she felt she'd already drunk more than enough. 'Will you excuse me for a moment?'

'Of course. I'll be over there by the fireplace,' he pointed to a small sofa pulled close to a blazing log fire. Chrissie nodded and headed for the powder room to check her make-up and ensure she hadn't got bits of chocolate Pavlova stuck to her teeth.

Trent waited until she was out of sight, then went swiftly in pursuit of James Hawksworth.

'James, can I have a quick word?'

'Of course. Can I buy you a drink?'

'No, thanks, Chrissie will be back in a minute.' He paused. 'It's about Chrissie, actually. I'm a little confused. I always understood that you were dead against her?'

'Not at all,' James denied promptly. 'In fact, I quite admire her. So does my wife,' he added quickly, afraid he sounded like a dirty old man. Trent frowned slightly.

'Yet am I right in thinking you sent Charles to Australia to split them up?'

'Partly, yes. The Australian trip had already been planned, and they were so young – far too young to consider marriage. Charles was barely eighteen, and Chrissie even younger. Mind you, I was proud of Charles for proposing marriage; most young men would have tried to take advantage of her situation...'

'Sorry, you've lost me,' Trent shook his head. 'What situation?'

'Well, her parents dying, and in such a traumatic way,' James said, then seeing that Trent still looked blank, clarified his remark. 'Of course, you weren't around here much at the time, but you must have heard about it. It even made the national press.'

'What did?' Trent tried to mask his impatience.

'A lorry driver, forget the chap's name, had a heart attack at the wheel, lost control and ploughed into a crowd of pedestrians,' James explained.

'Oh, that? My God. Chrissie's parents were involved?' he asked, appalled.

'Her mother was, killed outright, poor woman. Her father died a few days later; the shock triggered a stroke, if I remember correctly.'

'Oh, how dreadful for Chrissie,' Trent murmured. 'She can't have been more than a small child. I suppose that explains her craving for financial security,' he said, speaking more to himself than James. Explained it, certainly, did it also excuse it?

'What an odd thing to say,' James stared at him. And rather offensive, he thought, wondering why Trent had brought her out to dinner if he had such a low opinion of her. 'I never thought her mercenary, quite the opposite…' He paused, thinking back five years, then snapped his fingers at the sudden memory. 'Of course, I remember now. It caused quite a lot of bad feeling at the time…'

'What did?' Trent demanded, through gritted teeth.

'Well, the relatives of the other casualties were demanding compensation – something about the driver being forced to work more hours than he was supposed to without a break – but Chrissie refused to take anything. It made the others look bad, but she was adamant she wouldn't accept money in return for her mother's death.'

He smiled slightly. 'Only the very young can make such quixotic gestures. In fact, Sara and I tried to talk her out of it; she was very bright, academically, and had a place at university but she had to give that up and get a job. The compensation money would have funded her education and I'm sure her parents would have wanted her to take it, but she wouldn't,' he said, shaking his head at her obduracy.

'I wanted to help her find employment, but she was determined to do it on her own. Sara and I kept an eye on her for awhile, from a discreet distance, but she managed very well. She moved to a better job, bought a little house of her own... but you must already know most of this,' he broke off, and looked searchingly at Trent.

'Er, no, I'm afraid I didn't,' he mumbled. He couldn't remember when he had last felt so small; lower than a snake's belly. The things he had said to her, the accusations... How could he ever make it up to her?

'Are you sure you won't have a drink?' James offered again; he thought Trent looked in need of a stiff brandy.

'No, no thanks, I must go back to Chrissie,' he turned to leave, then paused. 'One more question, if I may? I don't suppose you'll have any objection if she and Charles are reconciled when he comes home?'

'None at all,' James said promptly.

'Thought not,' Trent muttered and, this time, he did leave the bar.

James watched him go, then realized that Charles might be treading on either Trent's or Ben's toes if he muscled in on Chrissie, and decided he'd better clarify matters. He didn't want his son making enemies as soon as he set foot back on English soil.

Trent couldn't find Chrissie anywhere. She wasn't by

the fire, although the tray of coffee had been placed on a low table. Could she still be in the cloakroom, maybe not feeling well?

'Excuse me,' he leaned over the reception desk. 'Could you please check the cloakroom for me? My… companion has been in there rather a long time.' He waited while the receptionist checked, but Chrissie was not in there. He looked around, feeling uneasy. Where was she?

Chrissie had seen Trent deep in conversation with James Hawksworth and hesitated over whether to join them. She hoped Trent wasn't warning James about her, telling him not to allow her within five miles of Charles, but she wouldn't put money on it.

Sighing, she turned and walked outside, feeling the need of some fresh air. The wine she had consumed had given her a slight headache and she had the depressing feeling that the evening was ruined; the mention of Charles Hawksworth's return had brought the suspicious, harsh expression back to Trent's face.

She breathed deeply as she strolled in the gardens and tried to convince herself she was being paranoid. After all, Trent had known James Hawksworth for years and they must have dozens of friends and acquaintances in common. They could be discussing any one of them and not be talking about her at all.

She was so deep in thought that she didn't hear the stealthy footsteps behind her, and wasn't aware of not being alone until a hand grabbed her arm.

'Trent…' she spun round, then her eyes widened in trepidation at the sight of the stranger who had accosted her. It was a young man of around her own age, clad in jeans and a grubby sweatshirt, his hair long and unkempt.

But it was the lustful gleam in his eyes and his aggressive stance that alerted her to the danger she had unwittingly walked into, and she swallowed nervously.

'No, not Trent!' he sneered. 'I suppose he's one of the rich bastards who own these flash cars!' He jerked his head towards the array of luxury models parked outside the hotel, and, for a moment, Chrissie hoped he was more interested in the cars than her.

'No, he's not,' she denied. 'He works here, we both do,' she lied, praying it was only the rich patrons he bore malice towards and not the workers. She suddenly jerked her captive arm backwards, hoping to take him by surprise and free herself, but he was too quick, too strong.

'No, you don't!' He tightened his grip, and Chrissie knew real, paralysing fear as he half-dragged, half-lifted her towards a clump of concealing bushes.

'Trent!' she screamed, and the man put one hand over her mouth to stifle her cries, while his other hand fondled her roughly. Then he tripped her, and she fell heavily to the ground.

Chrissie bit the hand covering her mouth and he swore, then dealt her a stinging blow across her face, cutting off her renewed attempt to call for help.

'*Bitch*! Lie still, or I'll really hurt you,' he threatened, but Chrissie barely heard him and wouldn't have obeyed even if she had.

She lashed out blindly with her fists and her feet. struggling wildly to be free of his oppressive weight, terror lending her extra strength as his hand tore at the front of her dress. This couldn't be happening! Not in a public place, with dozens of people only yards away!

Her breathing became ragged with fear and the realization of his superior strength, but then, suddenly and miraculously, he was lifted from her.

Trent, his eyes glittering ferociously in the half dark, shoved him hard against the trunk of a tree and slammed his fist into his stomach, doubling him over, then he hit him again before he could recover from the first blow. The crack of his knuckles against the younger man's jaw sounded sickeningly loud and Chrissie gasped, not sure whether it was Trent or the other who was hurt. She clutched her torn dress to her and staggered to her feet.

'Trent! That's enough!' It was James Hawksworth, his voice sharp and authoritative, his twenty years' experience of being a magistrate coming to the fore. If the beating continued, it would be Trent in trouble with the law, not the youth.

Trent paused, his fist still bunched in the assailant's sweatshirt, holding him captive, ready and more than willing to deal another, much harder blow.

'Trent!' It was James again and he stepped forward. 'I'll deal with this. You look after Chrissie,' he commanded. Some of the wild fury left Trent and he nodded and, somewhat reluctantly, released his hold, handing the youth over to James.

'Come on, sweetheart,' he said softly to Chrissie, and the gentleness in his voice was her undoing. Her lower lip wobbled and she blinked back tears.

'It's all right now,' he soothed her, as he picked up her bag and the jacket she had lost during the struggle. He put one strong arm around her and led her away, settling her into the car, tucking her jacket around her, then adding his own when he noticed her shivering.

He touched her hand briefly before starting up the engine and driving off, anxious to be away from the scene of the attack as quickly as possible.

Chrissie huddled silently in the passenger seat, half turned away from him so that he wouldn't see her tears. After a couple of minutes, Trent pulled into a lay-by and stilled the engine, then gently gathered her into his arms, half afraid of being rebuffed.

But she turned and buried her face in his shoulder and began to cry in earnest; harsh, racking sobs that tore at his heart. God, if he had accepted James's offer of a drink... His blood ran cold at the thought of what might have happened to Chrissie. And he was shamefully aware that nothing at all would have happened if he hadn't been checking up on her.

'Don't, please don't cry. It's over,' he murmured, stroking her hair back from her face and touching his lips to her hot tear-drenched cheek. It was a kiss to comfort and console, one that might be bestowed upon a hurt child, and Chrissie slowly began to relax into his safe embrace.

Eventually she was able to stop the tears, although an occasional shudder of revulsion shook her frame. But gradually her heartbeat slowed to a normal pace and her breathing became easier. Suddenly, achingly, she felt a great need for her mother's presence.

'I wish my mum was here,' she whispered, so softly Trent had to strain to hear her. His arms tightened protectively around her.

'I'm sorry, sweetheart, I can't do that for you,' he said regretfully. He had never used the phrase 'my mum' in his entire life, but it seemed perfectly natural to do so now. 'But I can offer you second-best. Would you like me to take you to *my* mum?' After a long pause, Chrissie nodded, slightly and almost imperceptibly, but it was still a nod of agreement.

'Let's go then,' he straightened and started up the car,

then punched out the number of Fairfax Hall on his mobile. 'Ma? I'm bringing Chrissie home, so have a room prepared for her, will you? What? No, she's upset; she'll want a hot bath and then straight to bed. We'll be with you in about ten minutes – I'll explain then,' he said, and punched the 'off' button.

He drove in silence, occasionally darting worried looks at an equally silent Chrissie. She was hunched away from him, as if he were her enemy, too, and he increased his speed, feeling she needed to be with a woman.

Celia had been watching out for them and hurried outside as soon as she saw the car's headlights approaching the house. Bright light spilled over the steps as she pulled open the front door.

'What is it? Have you had an accident?' she demanded of Trent, as he got out of the car and walked round to the passenger side.

'No questions yet, Ma, please. Some jerk assaulted Chrissie – she'll be all right, she's just shaken up,' he assured her quickly.

'Oh no!' Celia's hand went to her mouth and she bit back a cry of dismay when Trent helped Chrissie out of the car. The ripped dress and shredded tights told their own tale of violence and horror.

'You poor child,' she rushed over and hugged Chrissie, then slipped her arm around her waist to support her. Chrissie began limping towards the house, then stopped and looked down at the ground.

'I've lost a shoe,' she said, in a high-pitched voice unlike her own.

'I'll go back for it,' Trent offered quickly.

'No!' she interrupted. 'I never want to see it again.' She pulled at her dress in distaste, the dress she had bought to attract Trent's admiration of her body. Another shudder racked her and she was suddenly afraid that she might be sick. 'I'll never wear any of this again. I'll burn it all!' She stopped, and put a hand to her head, swaying dizzily. Her headache had returned with a vengeance.

'Trent,' Celia motioned for him to carry her indoors, a little surprised he hadn't already done so. He hesitated, half expecting her to shy away from a man's touch, but she made no demur when he swung her up into his arms and carried her up the stairs.

'I've prepared the guest room next to mine,' Celia told him, hurrying along beside him. 'The electric blanket is on and there's plenty of hot water.'

'Good.' He lowered Chrissie gently to her feet on the threshold of the room and immediately stepped back on to the landing. 'Look after her, Ma. I have to make a couple of phone calls.' He looked searchingly at Chrissie, but she had her head averted. He reached out and touched her lightly on the hand. 'You're safe now. Try to relax,' he said gently. 'I'll see you tomorrow.'

Chrissie nodded. She knew she ought to thank him for rescuing her, and Celia for welcoming an unexpected house guest, but talking, or moving, was suddenly too much of an effort. Tomorrow. I'll thank them tomorrow, she thought wearily.

'I'll run your bath,' Celia said. 'Come and sit over here until it's ready,' she added, leading Chrissie by the hand over to an armchair beside the bed. Chrissie vaguely registered that it was a very pretty room, in shades of cream and gold.

'Thank you,' she finally managed to speak, sitting where she had been told. She was glad to have the bath prepared for her and waited, like a small child, to be told when it was ready.

'Can you manage?' Celia asked anxiously. 'Have a long soak and I'll be back shortly, with a hot drink and something to wear.'

'Thank you,' Chrissie said again. Left alone, she peeled off her clothes and, grimacing distastefully, kicked them aside. She climbed into the hot, soapy water and winced slightly as the broken skin of her arms and legs began to sting.

She tried to force herself to relax but, behind her closed lids she could see *him*, his lascivious face intent on rape… She sat up with a start, sloshing water over the side of the tub, her heart beating rapidly with fear. She concentrated on breathing deeply while repeatedly telling herself that it was over, and she was safe. But she knew it would be a long time until she forgot the terror of those moments before Trent rescued her, and she began soaping herself vigorously, as if she could scrub away the memory of her assailant's hurting hands and cruel intent.

She was out of the bath and wrapped in a large towel when Celia returned, carrying a night-dress, dressing-gown and toiletries. Celia masked her horror at seeing the welts on Chrissie's body and smiled warmly.

'Come and sit down, and I'll put antiseptic on those scratches,' she said briskly. Chrissie sat stoically while Celia dabbed away with cotton wool.

'Trent's taken Molly over to your cottage to collect some clothes, and Molly will drive your car back so that it's here when you want it,' she told her.

'Thank you,' Chrissie managed a smile.

'But please stay for as long as you want to,' Celia urged her. 'You mustn't go home while you're the slightest bit afraid of being alone. I'd love having you to stay,' she said, with obvious sincerity. Chrissie felt tears well up and blinked them away.

'You're very kind,' she managed.

'Not at all. It's lovely to have someone to fuss over. Trent and Ben won't let me,' she added regretfully. 'Now, put this nightie on and get into bed,' she said, and herself popped the night-gown over Chrissie's head, as if she were indeed a little girl. Then she tucked her into bed and piled pillows behind her shoulders.

The bed was wonderfully warm and comfortable, and Chrissie stretched her legs out.

'I'll be back in a minute,' Celia said, and bustled out. She was as quick as she'd said and reappeared with a tray containing a pot of hot chocolate and a plate of biscuits. Chrissie declined the latter, but sipped gratefully at the hot, soothing liquid.

'Trent said I was to give you one of my sleeping pills,' Celia said next, handing over a small tablet. Chrissie looked at it dubiously. 'They're very mild, and he checked with our doctor – he said it was perfectly safe for you to take one, just this once. It will ensure you get a good night's sleep,' she said firmly.

'All right, thank you,' Chrissie said.

'I meant what I said, about you staying here,' Celia sat down on the side of the bed and reached for Chrissie's hand. 'It would be like having a daughter...' she broke off, obviously upset.

'Are you thinking about Francesca?' Chrissie asked, feeling she must be already on the road to recovery if her curiosity about Trent's wife was again on her mind. But Celia shook her head.

'No, I didn't see much of Francesca, really. They lived in London. No, I was thinking of my own...' she smiled sadly. 'She was stillborn. It was almost twenty-seven years ago, but I think about her all the time. I wonder what she'd look like, would she be married and have children of her own…'

'I'm so sorry,' Chrissie squeezed her hand sympathetically. She couldn't imagine how it must feel, to lose a child. Celia smiled, berating herself for the untimely confidence. Really, she was supposed to be comforting Chrissie, not the other way around!

'It was a long time ago. Now, drink up, swallow that pill and snuggle down,' she instructed. 'I'm not going to badger you with questions, but I'm here to listen if you want to talk about it. My room's next door, if you wake during the night, but I think you'll sleep like a baby.'

'Yes,' Chrissie obediently swallowed the sedative with the last of her hot chocolate, and slid down beneath the sheets.

'You'll feel much better about things tomorrow, I promise,' Celia told her. She bent and kissed Chrissie's cheek, then straightened. 'I'll leave one lamp on. Goodnight, dear,' she snapped out the overhead light and left the room.

'Goodnight,' Chrissie echoed into the darkness and lay quietly for awhile, but soon the drug worked its soothing magic and she fell into a deep and dreamless slumber.

chapter eleven

Trent quietly opened the door and left it ajar as he stepped noiselessly into the room and carefully placed the suitcase Molly had packed at the foot of the bed.

He could see Chrissie was sleeping peacefully: she was lying perfectly still on her side, her hands tucked beneath her chin, lashes fanning her cheeks, and her hair spreading out on the pillow like a golden halo. She did indeed look angelic, he thought, then smiled slightly. No, she had too much spirit ever to be described as an angel! And it was that spirit which would enable her to recover from her ordeal. At least, he hoped so.

He stayed watching her, as if on guard duty, until the incongruity of that particular thought hit him with the force of a hammer blow. Yeah, sure, it's me she needs protecting from, he thought, full of shame.

He was no better than the lout who had attacked her. They had both wanted the same thing from her, the only difference being that he, Trent, would have been more subtle about it, wooing her first, plying her with champagne and seducing her in one of the White Hart's four-poster beds.

His intentions towards her had been no more honourable than those of her assailant. He had believed her to be – on flimsy evidence and half-remembered gossip – a gold-digger, and therefore easy prey for a man of his wealth. He should stick to women of his own age, mostly divorcees or career women who knew the score.

They weren't looking for marriage or children, merely an enjoyable, but temporary, sexual relationship with no strings.

'Trent,' Celia whispered from the open doorway. 'James Hawksworth is on the phone.' He nodded, and with one last, regretful look at the girl he had misjudged and treated so badly, he turned and left the room.

Celia watched him go, puzzled by the forbidding expression and taut lines etched on his face, but encouraged by having found him in Chrissie's room. Perhaps this horrible attack on Chrissie would prove to be the catalyst needed to jolt Trent into admitting his feelings, acknowledging his need to allow someone back into his life and his heart.

Chrissie awoke abruptly, confused by her unfamiliar surroundings until the events of the night before flooded back, when she had to bite her lip hard to stop herself crying out.

Her panic slowly subsided and she noticed that someone had brought in a breakfast tray containing orange juice, croissants and coffee. She placed her hand against the coffee pot and snatched it away immediately; it was piping hot, so whoever had brought it in had only just been and gone. That must have been what had awoken her.

She picked up the glass of orange juice and drank thirstily, then pushed back the covers, padded over to the window and pulled back the drapes. Warm sunlight poured into the room and she gazed out at the extensive grounds of Fairfax Hall. It was a quiet, peaceful scene, and she realized that the long, drug-induced sleep had done its healing work. She had to be positive, not dwell on what had happened but be thankful that it had been no worse, she told herself firmly, turning back to help herself to food and coffee.

It was then that she noticed her suitcase, pounced on it and opened it up. Molly had packed several changes of clothing and Chrissie picked out underwear, a plain black skirt and lilac sweater. She was relieved to note that there was no sign of the clothes she had worn the night before; someone had discreetly removed them – and burned them, she hoped.

After breakfast, she showered, dressed and put on some make-up, then felt ready to face the world, and left the room. The other bedroom doors were closed and she resisted the urge to peek, to try to discover which one belonged to Trent.

She carried her breakfast tray down to the kitchen and found a girl she'd never seen before washing up.

'Can I help?' Chrissie asked, smiling.

'Oh no, miss,' she seemed shocked by the suggestion. 'Mrs Fairfax is in the library,' she added.

'Thanks.' Chrissie could take a hint. She retraced her steps and entered the library. Celia was reading the papers in front of the fire, but put them aside at once and studied Chrissie's face intently.

'Come and sit down and have some coffee. How are you feeling this morning?'

'Much better, thank you.' Chrissie took the chair opposite, but declined the offer of coffee.

'You certainly look rested,' Celia nodded approvingly, then reached across and patted her hand. 'Now, it's nothing for you to worry about, but James Hawksworth is coming here to talk to you.'

'Oh no,' Chrissie frowned. She didn't actually want to

remember anything about the attack, but she could recall Mr Hawksworth saying he would deal with her assailant while Trent took her home.

'Did he report it to the police?' she asked, but already knew the answer. James Hawksworth was a magistrate, which was why he had stopped Trent from continuing the beating he had begun. She put a hand to her cheek, still slightly red and swollen from the heavy slap she had received, and knew which brand of justice she preferred. And it wasn't James Hawksworth's!

'Yes, he had to, dear, didn't he?' Celia said gently.

Chrissie didn't agree, so changed the subject to one of more importance to her. 'Where's Trent?' she asked.

'Oh,' Celia couldn't meet her gaze. 'I'm afraid he had to return to London,' she said regretfully. 'Pressure of work, you know. But he was insistent you should stay here and let us look after you,' she added warmly. Chrissie forced a smile. Why had he gone, without a word? Or even a note, if he'd had to leave early and didn't want to wake her? she wondered sadly.

Celia was almost as upset as Chrissie by his departure: her high hopes of last night had been dashed when he had curtly announced his intention of leaving first thing in the morning. She was sure in her heart that he had strong feelings for Chrissie, but was beginning to despair of him ever admitting it, even to himself.

'Oh, here's James now,' Celia glanced out of the window at the sound of tyres on gravel, and went to meet him.

Chrissie stayed where she was, feeling absurdly embarrassed at having to face him. His last sight of her, sprawled on the ground... She shuddered. Stop it! she admonished herself. You did nothing wrong, you have nothing to be ashamed of, or embarrassed about.

She still found it hard to meet his eyes when he followed Celia into the library, but as he was, unfortunately, accustomed to dealing with victims of sexual crime in the magistrates' court, he was able to deal with the matter calmly and matter-of-factly, though with compassion.

'How are you, Chrissie?' he asked, with a warm smile.

'I'll be OK ,' she nodded. 'But…I don't want to press charges; I couldn't bear to go to court, to see him…' Her voice rose slightly, and she stopped speaking.

'I understand,' James said soothingly. 'Trent thought you would feel that way. We've both told the police what happened. The young man…'

'I don't want to even know his name,' Chrissie interrupted; somehow, that would make it even more real.

'Very well. But let me just assure you that he's not a local man, so you're unlikely ever to come across him again. He has a criminal record, mostly for car crime. His fingerprints have been found on a car stolen in Birmingham yesterday; it ran out of petrol amile or so from the White Hart. He's admitted he was there looking for a replacement …'

'It's a pity he didn't find one!' Celia burst out. Talk about being in the wrong place at the wrong time. A few minutes earlier or later, and Chrissie would never have been attacked. 'Chrissie doesn't have to talk to the police, does she?'

'Not if she doesn't want to press charges,' James said, much to Chrissie's relief. She couldn't bear to talk about it with strangers, particularly male strangers, asking why she had been alone, what had she been wearing, had she encouraged him… Oh no!

'They've charged him with several offences relating to vehicle crime, and he's due in court on Monday morning,' James continued. 'With his record, he's almost certain to get a custodial sentence.'

'Good,' Celia nodded approvingly.

'Is there anything I can do for you, Chrissie?' James asked her.

'No, thank you,' she said politely. 'I'm grateful for your help; it was lucky you were there,' she added, rather insincerely. He had meant well, of course, and he had helped her, but she wished the police had been left out of it.

'Yes. Trent could have been in a lot of trouble if I hadn't been there,' James told her, rather sternly, as if he guessed her thoughts. Both Chrissie and Celia looked up sharply.

'He could? But why?' Chrissie protested. 'He was defending me.'

'He went further than that. And would have done more if I hadn't stopped him,' he added reprovingly. He noted Chrissie and Celia bore almost identical expressions of 'Good for Trent!' and decided to drop the subject. He understood their attitude, though he couldn't condone it.

After James had left, Chrissie went outside for some fresh air. Oscar, Ben's collie, was lying outside Ben's door but padded over to her when he saw her, tail wagging a welcome. He kept her company while she strolled and she threw tennis balls for him to chase and retrieve. She enjoyed herself. She would have loved a dog of her own, but it didn't seem fair to leave one alone while she was out at work all day.

The fresh air and exercise relieved much of her pent-up tension and she felt much more relaxed when she went back indoors. She had also developed a healthy appetite, and the delicious aroma of roasting chicken made her mouth water in anticipation.

Molly turned from the Aga and smiled at her.

'Your timing's spot on,' she said. 'Lunch is almost ready. Your legs are younger than mine, so would you run upstairs and tell Celia? She's in her bedroom.'

'Sure.' Chrissie went through to the hall and then ran up the stairs, and knocked lightly at the door of the room next to the one she had used.

'Come in, dear,' Celia was writing letters at a small desk placed in the sun-filled window alcove. 'Did you enjoy your walk?'

'Yes, thank you. Molly says to tell you lunch is almost ready.'

'Good. I've finished here.' Celia stacked envelopes into a loose pile to be posted later.

One fell on to the carpet and Chrissie moved forward to pick it up.

As she placed it back on the desk, she froze, for she was staring at a silver-framed photograph of Trent on his wedding day. He looked young, carefree and happy, as proud as any bridegroom could be. The radiant girl clutching his arm was one of the most beautiful creatures Chrissie had ever seen. She was small and slender, with masses of midnight-black hair framing a perfect oval face which was dominated by huge, liquid brown eyes, eyes that were full of adoration as she gazed up at her handsome new husband.

'Francesca,' Chrissie whispered.

'Yes. I keep it up here so Trent won't see it and be upset,' Celia said awkwardly. She wished Chrissie hadn't seen it, either.

'She was beautiful,' Chrissie sighed wistfully. Her own

blonde prettiness seemed ordinary in comparison to Francesca's exotic beauty.

'Yes.'

'What I don't understand,' Chrissie began slowly, 'is why he didn't go after her?'

'Go after her?!' Celia was alarmed. 'Whatever do you mean by that?'

'Well,' Chrissie was taken aback by Celia's reaction. 'He still wears his wedding ring, so I always assumed she left him, not the other way round. I can't imagine Trent standing by and letting her do that. Was…was there another man involved?' she asked, though it seemed a ludicrous question. How any woman in her right mind would want to leave Trent Fairfax for someone else was beyond her comprehension.

'Oh no, it was nothing like that. Chrissie, I thought you knew…? Francesca died,' Celia told her.

'Died?' Chrissie stared at her, stricken. '*Oh, no*! I…I said some dreadful things to him,' she whispered, trying to recall the exact words she had flung at him that night in the cottage, when he had reacted so violently to her taunting. She had told him he deserved to lose his wife, she remembered wretchedly; in fact, hadn't she more or less accused him of being responsible for what had happened in his marriage?

'Oh my God,' she moaned, covering her eyes with her hands in horror at what she had done. 'He must think I'm the most callous, unfeeling…'

'You can put it right,' Celia said urgently.

'How?' Chrissie dropped her hands and stared at her hopefully.

'Do you love him?' Celia asked. It wasn't what Chrissie had been expecting to hear, but she didn't have to think twice before answering.

'Yes. Oh, yes I do!' she declared fervently. Celia smiled her relief.

'Then go to him,' she said simply.

'I will.' Again Chrissie didn't need time to consider and began to run from the room.

'Chrissie!'

'What?' She half-turned, impatient to be on her way.

'Do you know his address?' Celia was busily writing it down as she spoke.

'Um…no,' Chrissie admitted, feeling a little foolish, and retraced her steps. She took the piece of paper from Celia's outstretched hand.

'Good luck. I'll be praying for you,' Celia stood up and embraced her, then let her go.

'Molly! Where did you put my car keys?' Chrissie called, as she raced down the stairs.

'They're in the ignition,' Molly said, appearing from the kitchen. 'Where are you going? Lunch is… ready,' she finished and shrugged her shoulders. The front door had already slammed behind Chrissie.

Upstairs, Celia crossed swiftly to the window overlooking the drive and watched the blue Mini roar off. She hoped she'd done the right thing, urging the girl to follow Trent. She had been so sure he reciprocated Chrissie's feelings – until he'd disappeared to London this morning, without waiting to see her first, or even leaving a message.

She didn't understand that at all. It was true he had asked her to take care of Chrissie, but she had made up the excuse of him having to go because of pressure of work. Trent hadn't given any reason for his sudden departure. She hoped she wasn't sending Chrissie on a fool's errand, and wondered if she ought to phone Trent? She decided not to; she had probably meddled enough and, besides, the unexpectedness of Chrissie's arrival might jolt him into dropping his guard.

Chrissie parked her car, somewhat haphazardly, at Farminster railway station, and dashed inside. She knew trains left every hour during the week, but couldn't remember the weekend timetable.

'When's the next train to London?' she demanded, grabbing a man wearing a blue blazer. He wasn't actually a member of staff, but he helped her anyway, sensing her urgency and unable to resist the appeal in her large, violet eyes.

She was in luck, and barely had time to buy her ticket and clamber aboard before the train pulled out. It was only then, when she was on her way and had time to think, that doubt crept in and she began to wonder at the wisdom of her action. But she had to see him. It was as simple as that. If he didn't want to see her, well, she'd have to deal with that later. But she had to tell him she hadn't known he had been widowed.

The journey seemed endless but was finally over, and she joined a short queue for a taxi; it was quite beyond her to interpret the underground map or waste precious time hanging about for buses.

She clutched the piece of paper bearing his address as if it were a talisman: his mother had wanted her to come, so she must have believed Trent would welcome her. She clung to that hope and fought down the beginnings of panic as she got into a cab and gave the address.

Her legs were shaking with nerves as she paid the driver and climbed out, gazing up at the large house where Trent's flat was located. She walked up the steps and studied the brass name plates. She took a deep breath, offered up a silent prayer and pressed the buzzer for 'Fairfax'.

There was no response. She bit her lip and tried again, but to no avail. What an anti-climax! She sighed and sat down on the top step, determined to wait. She had come this far and she certainly wasn't going back home until she had seen him.

An hour later, she was still waiting and was shivering with cold. She had dashed out without a coat and it had begun to drizzle, slowly but relentlessly. She began to walk up and down in an effort to keep warm, venturing only twenty yards from the house in one direction before turning and walking twenty yards in the other, to ensure she didn't miss him when he appeared. *If* he appeared.

Perhaps he was at his office – wherever that was? she thought glumly. She could go and phone Celia to find out, but then I'd probably miss him while he was on his way home, she thought dispiritedly. Why on earth hadn't she telephoned him first? But she already knew the answer to that; it was because she had been afraid he'd tell her not to come.

I'm staying, she decided resolutely; he has to come home sooner or later. By now, her hair was plastered to her skull, her skirt and sweater were clinging damply and unpleasantly to her skin, and she was attracting attention.

She tried to ignore it, and told herself nothing could happen to her in broad daylight on a Saturday afternoon. But the memory of the night before was stronger than reason; every innocent passer-by became a potential attacker and she was struggling to contain a rising panic when Trent finally strolled – yes, strolled! – into view.

He hadn't been working either, she noticed at once. He

was in casual clothes and trainers, and was carrying a gym bag with the handle of a squash racket sticking out.

'You've been at the gym!' she accused him hotly. Trent had been deep in thought and he blinked at her, not sure he hadn't conjured her up out of his imagination. But no, this furious impersonator of a drowned rat was definitely not the angelically-sleeping Chrissie he had been thinking about all day, even while beating the hell out of a squash ball or attempting to rid himself of his self-loathing by thumping the punch-bag as if he were hitting himself.

'Yes, I have.' It was all he could think of to say. They just stood and looked at each other for a moment, then Trent pulled himself together and fished out his keys.

'You're shivering; you'd better come in and dry off. And then you can tell me why you're here,' he added. There was no discernible emotion in his voice, neither pleasure at seeing her, but no irritation either, she thought, following him silently into the ground floor flat.

Chrissie stood in the living room, surreptitiously looking around. She was pleased to note that it was a very masculine room; there was no fuss or frills, but huge leather armchairs and sturdy tables, plain lamps and even plainer furnishings. She felt sure Francesca had never lived here with him.

'Here,' Trent tossed her a towel. 'Dry your hair or you'll catch your death,' he said casually, as he moved across the room to switch on the gas fire. Death. Chrissie licked her lips, then drew a deep breath.

'I had to come. I didn't know Francesca had died, until today. I thought you were divorced and I said some truly dreadful things to you, implying you were to blame. I know you spoke of her in the past tense, but divorced men do that, don't they? They say she was bad-tempered, or was extravagant, not *is*, because their ex-wife's faults and foibles don't concern them any more...' She finally ran out of breath and took a huge gulp of air. Trent's face was unreadable.

'You're obviously spending too much time with my mother,' he said finally, calmly. 'You're beginning to babble just like she does.'

'Trent! Don't,' Chrissie held one hand out to him pleadingly. 'I feel really bad about the things I said. I've come all this way to apologize.'

'I know. It wasn't necessary,' he said coolly. 'Come and sit by the fire to dry your clothes. Would you like a brandy to warm you up?'

'Yes, please,' she said, although she felt that she needed it more for Dutch courage than for warmth. The centrally heated flat was cosy enough without the added heat from the fire, but she knelt down in front of it and began rubbing her hair with the towel.

She took the brandy he held out to her and sat back on her heels, sipping it slowly, and watching him from beneath lowered lashes. Celia had asked her if she loved him. Until that moment, she hadn't realized that she did, and now the knowledge both exhilarated and frightened her. She sensed that what she said and did now would impact on the rest of her life.

She gained a tiny bit of confidence from seeing that he had helped himself to some brandy too. Unless he was a regular afternoon tippler, which she doubted, perhaps he wasn't quite as composed and self-assured as he seemed to be.

He was sitting in one of the leather chairs to the side of the fireplace, and Chrissie placed her empty glass down on the marble hearth, then moved a little closer to him.

'Will you tell me about Francesca?' she asked softly. 'I saw a photograph of her; she was lovely.'

'Yes, she was,' Trent said, after a moment. 'I met her in Rome, when I was doing business with her father. She was…different. Before her, I'd dated career-minded girls at university, or spoilt little rich girls…'

'Not like Annabel?' Chrissie couldn't help but interrupt. He slanted her a slight smile.

'I'm afraid so. They were bright, fun people who loved the social whirl, but thought of little other than clothes, parties and holidays. I always grew bored with them very quickly. Francesca wasn't like them at all. She had never even set foot in a night-club and hadn't been brought up to consider having a career. All she wanted was to be a wife and mother. She had half a dozen nephews and nieces, and adored spending her time with them.'

'Did you love her very much?' Chrissie had to ask, but could hardly bear to hear the answer.

'Yes,' he said quietly, gazing down into his empty glass. 'And she loved me.' Chrissie bit down hard on her lower lip. Why had she tortured herself by asking? 'But we made each other miserable,' he added harshly. Chrissie's head jerked up.

'Miserable?'

'Yes. She hated living in England, hated being away from her family, and either couldn't or wouldn't under-stand why I needed to work such long hours. I was in danger of going bankrupt; I was badly over-extended, millions of pounds in debt…'

'Didn't you tell her?'

'No, she wasn't interested in business.' He shook his head dismissively. Neither are Ben or your mother, Chrissie thought; she would bet that he'd never told them he was in financial trouble.

'I introduced her to my friends,' he continued, 'but she hated them, too. She was shocked by the promiscuity of the single women... and some of the married ones, too,' he grimaced. 'She became aware that there was a lot of adultery going on, and began to be suspicious.' He sighed, remembering the groundless accusations he'd had to listen to after a sixteen-hour working day.

If the women were anything like Annabel Harrington-Smyth, Chrissie could understand why she'd been worried, but she kept silent.

'She became obsessed with getting pregnant,' Trent continued. 'And each month, the obsession grew. It got so bad that she couldn't see the point in making love if it wasn't likely to result in conception,' he said, rather moodily. 'Then, she *did* become pregnant,' he said. Chrissie gasped, but he didn't hear her; he was lost in the past.

'I was pleased, more for her than for myself. I thought she'd be happy once the baby was born. But she had a difficult pregnancy, right from the start. Then there were problems with high blood pressure and she had to be hospitalized. It seemed to be under control, and she was allowed home for the weekend.' He stopped, and took a deep, shuddering breath before continuing.

'I woke up suddenly in the middle of the night, and she was having some sort of fit, and screaming...' He closed his eyes against the memory. 'The ambulance arrived quickly and they got her stabilized. She was seven months pregnant and I was told the best chance for both her and the baby was an emergency Caesarean. I gave permission and they took her straight down to surgery, but... I lost them both,' he finished bleakly. Chrissie didn't say anything, but reached up and touched his cheek.

He grabbed her hand and held it so tightly she thought her fingers would be crushed, but she didn't dream of pulling away. Trent gazed down into her eyes, soft and dark with unspoken compassion and he smiled slightly.

'Thanks for not telling me it wasn't my fault. I grew sick of hearing that.'

'You already know it wasn't your fault,' she said. 'At least, in your head you know it.' She reached up with her other hand and lightly touched his temple. 'But perhaps you still don't know it in your heart,' she added, moving her hand to his chest.

'Such wisdom in one so young,' he said, though rather mockingly, she thought.

'I know a lot about feeling guilty when someone dies,' she told him quietly.

'You do?' Trent frowned. 'Who?'

'My mum,' she replied, after a long pause.

'James Hawksworth told me that she was killed in a traffic accident; how can you shoulder any blame for what happened?' he asked gently.

'It was my fault she was in town that day, that's how. She asked me to run some errands for her after school, but I couldn't be bothered,' Chrissie said bitterly. 'I wanted to do something else, something vitally important like hanging around the shopping arcade with my friends! If I hadn't been so selfish, she'd have been safe at home and nowhere near that lorry…'

'Oh, Chrissie,' Trent reached down and lifted her on to his lap, as he might a distressed child. He knew, only too well, the futility of well-meaning platitudes, and said nothing more, but gathered her close. Chrissie clutched his sweater and nestled close, deriving comfort from the strength of his arms around her.

Trent gazed down at her; her eyes were closed, lashes spiky with unshed tears, her mouth full and slightly trembling. Even as he told himself he shouldn't, he bent his mouth to hers, prepared to pull away if she resisted him. But she didn't; she responded hungrily, her arms went up and around his neck to pull him even closer. Her mouth opened beneath his and she moaned, deep in her throat when his tongue tangled with hers, and she pressed her body against his.

chapter twelve

'No…' Trent broke away abruptly, and pulled her arms from around his neck.

'No?' Chrissie came back to earth with a bump and stared at him in consternation. 'I don't understand. I thought you wanted me.'

'I did. I do. Dammit, Chrissie, why do you think I left you safely with my mother and came back here?' he asked harshly.

'I've no idea,' she said simply, gazing at him with guile-less, innocent eyes.

'Because I was ashamed,' he ground out. 'I planned to seduce you last night. I deliberately chose the White Hart because it's a luxury hotel as well as a restaurant. I was going to ply you with champagne and compliments, kisses and caresses…'

'I expect I'd have enjoyed that,' Chrissie interrupted, with a demure smile. Trent looked at her sharply, then grabbed her shoulders.

'Don't you understand what I'm telling you? I didn't have a ring in my pocket, or a flowery proposal speech prepared. I've tried marriage and kids, and it was a disaster I have no intention of repeating. Chrissie, all I had planned for you was one night, one perfect night…' He stopped and swallowed. 'Because of me, you were attacked…'

'It wasn't your fault,' Chrissie protested.

'Wasn't it?' His mouth twisted.

'No, how could it be? Because you chose to take me to the White Hart?'

'No,' he shook his head. 'That lout wouldn't have approached you while you were with me. But I left you alone, didn't I? Do you want to know what I was doing?'

'I saw you talking to James Hawksworth,' Chrissie said.

'I was checking up on you,' he said baldly. 'I didn't understand his friendliness towards you, particularly with Charles coming home. I've always been under the impression he was against your relationship.'

'He was.'

'But not because he disliked you, or mistrusted your motives. Quite the opposite; he admires you. He told me you refused to accept compensation for your mother's death,' he added. Chrissie looked away.

'You know why I did that.'

'Yes.'

'Do you trust me now?' she asked softly. 'Or do you still think I'm interested in your money?'

'I trust you,' he said, unhesitatingly.

'Then believe me when I say I love...'

'No!' he interrupted. She ignored him.

'If one night,' she took a deep breath, 'if one perfect night is all you can offer me, then I accept...'

'No,' he said again. 'If I took you to bed, I'd be as much of a bastard as that yob who...'

'No.' It was Chrissie's turn to interrupt. 'I know what you're telling me, and I understand your reasons. I won't make demands on you. Let me stay. I want to forget that pig ever touched me. You can make me forget, I know you can,' she said softly.

'Chrissie,' Trent groaned, and gathered her to him. 'I ought to send you home,' he muttered, but he knew his voice lacked conviction. Chrissie knew it, too, and pressed home her advantage.

'I can't leave now. It would be dark by the time I got back to Farminster,' she protested. 'Anyone could be hanging around the station car park,' she added, and didn't have to feign fear of travelling alone at night.

'I'll drive you home,' he offered.

'And leave me to spend the night alone in my cottage?'

'I'll take you back to my mother,' he said next, rather desperately.

'I don't think she'd be very pleased to see me – she told me to come to you.'

'She did?' Trent raised one dark eyebrow. Chrissie nodded. 'You can stay in my guest room,' he decided.

'All right,' Chrissie agreed, rather too demurely. Trent shot her a look of suspicion. Did she even guess how hard it was for him to resist her? He could fight his own base instincts – just – but not if he had to fight her, as well.

'We'll go out this evening…' he began, thinking he wouldn't have to fight so hard in public. Just then, Chrissie's tummy rumbled, loudly and unromantically. 'Are you hungry?' he asked.

There was no point in denying it. 'I'm starving,' she admitted. 'I didn't have any lunch.'

'But you've had a large brandy,' Trent reminded her. 'Come on into the kitchen. Molly put some provisions in my car but I haven't unpacked the boxes yet,' he said, leading the way into a small but well-fitted kitchen. The units and cupboards, a stark white, were not to Chrissie's taste, but she was too hungry to notice her surroundings.

'Does she think you can't buy "proper" food in London?' she asked, busily taking lids off airtight containers to check the contents.

'Probably,' he said dryly. 'Tea? Or coffee?'

'Tea would be lovely,' Chrissie said absently, more interested in a home-made crusty loaf and raisin scones. Trent switched on the kettle, then silently placed crockery, cutlery, butter, cheese and jam in front of her.

'I'll go and change while you eat,' he said easily, feeling he was back in control now. 'Make yourself at home.'

'Trent?'

'Yes?' he paused.

'Did you and Francesca live here?' she asked, diffidently, wanting to be sure. He smiled slightly.

'No,' he said quietly. Chrissie nodded and smiled back, then returned her attention to the food.

Trent had showered before leaving the gym, so now he quickly shaved and changed his clothes. He booked a table for dinner, then checked his watch. There was something else he wanted to do first, but it was getting late. He returned to the kitchen where Chrissie was polishing off a huge slice of Molly's fudge-topped chocolate cake.

'We're going shopping,' he announced. 'I want to replace the outfit you were wearing last night.' He held up a hand when she began to protest that it wasn't necessary. 'Don't argue, please. It's the least I can do, and it will make me feel slightly better about what happened. Besides, I'm taking you out later,' he added.

'Oh,' Chrissie glanced down at her skirt and sweater. 'OK,' she agreed happily. He had stopped talking about sending her home, so she wouldn't object if he suggested they spend the evening pushing a trolley round the supermarket.

'If you've had enough to eat, I'll get us a cab,' he said, rather dryly, Chrissie thought, as if he were afraid she would eat him out of house and home.

'I was hungry,' she protested, hastily sweeping bread crumbs into her palm. Was it her fault if fresh, crusty loaves crumbled all over the place when sliced?

'I wasn't complaining,' he assured her truthfully. It felt good to see her in his rather sterile kitchen, making the place look homely for once. 'Come on, or we'll be too late,' he said, more briskly.

They went to a boutique in Knightsbridge which sold underwear and accessories as well as outer garments. Trent hoped Chrissie hadn't noticed the manageress greet him by name. However she had, and shot him a sideways glance.

'I suppose you're going to tell me you buy your mother's birthday and Christmas gifts here?' she commented, rather tartly.

'Would you believe me?' he asked. Chrissie glanced at the rails of lingerie and dresses aimed for the younger market and shook her head.

'No.'

'How about that lavender silk?' he suggested hastily.

His choice was perfect for her, the colour highlighted the violet of her eyes and the material draped softly over her curves. Tiny embroidered flowers of purple and lilac dotted the neckline and spaghetti straps. Chrissie loved it, and searched for a price tag.

'Go and try it on,' Trent diverted her attention. He knew she wouldn't find a ticket. In this establishment, if you had to ask the price, you couldn't afford it. 'You'll need a jacket or coat,' he said, and riffled through the selection on offer, choosing a loose-fitting silk jacket in a darker shade of lavender.

'Well?' Chrissie pirouetted for his approval.

'Wonderful,' he declared, taking out his credit card

while she disappeared back into the changing room. He had seen her eyeing a pale pink suede suit and asked the manageress if it would fit Chrissie.

'Oh yes, she's a perfect size ten,' he was assured, so he promptly added it to his purchases. He didn't tell Chrissie, though.

'I'll need make-up,' Chrissie rummaged through her bag once they were outside and discovered she had only a comb and lip gloss.

'No, you don't,' he told her firmly. 'You have beautiful skin and gorgeous eyes…' He stopped, remembering with difficulty his platonic intentions for the evening.

'Do I?' Chrissie asked eagerly.

'You know you do. Stop fishing for compliments,' he rebuked her.

'Can I just buy some mascara?' she wheedled.

'OK,' he relented.

It had begun to rain again by the time Chrissie had bought what she needed and they headed back to Trent's flat. Chrissie thought her towel-dried hair looked awful and asked if she could shampoo it before they went to dinner.

'Sure.' Trent showed her to the bathroom. She had to change clothes, too, he realized. God, would she take a shower, or have a bath? He couldn't trust himself to stay if she did…

'Help yourself to whatever you need; I have to go out for a while. Work…' he explained vaguely, and shot out of the flat at a rate of knots. Walking the streets in the rain cooled his ardour a bit, but not much, and Chrissie, stunning in the lavender silk when he returned, sent his blood pressure soaring.

'Dinner,' he said firmly.

'Good. I'm hungry again,' she confessed happily.

'So am I,' he muttered, but he wasn't thinking of food.

They ate at an Italian restaurant in Covent Garden, then went on to a night-club. It wasn't Trent's scene, but he wanted the excuse to hold her in his arms and enjoy the sensuous movements of her body against his. He was still telling himself that he wouldn't take her to bed: slow dancing, kissing in the safety of a public place was the most he would admit to wanting from her.

Chrissie was on a high, almost as if she were drunk, yet she had consumed very little alcohol. Being held by him, having him smile and joke, and drop soft kisses on her shoulders or temple, or, occasionally, her mouth… It was all a wonderful dream. She was falling more deeply in love with him with every passing minute, and her excitement grew with every touch, every kiss and she wanted to be alone with him. Now! She wasn't quite brave enough to suggest it, though, but the arrival of a large, noisy, drunken party of revellers made leaving a mutual decision.

As they got out of the cab and climbed the steps to the flat, Chrissie's heart was beating like a drum with anticipation of what might happen. Trent unlocked the door and ushered her inside, pausing in the hallway while he battled with his baser instincts. He won – briefly.

'This is the guest bedroom,' he told her, opening the door.

'So it is,' Chrissie spared it a brief glance as she walked past.

'Are you sure about this?' Trent gave her one last chance to change her mind.

'I'm sure,' she smiled tremulously, a little afraid. Not of him, but of disappointing him, fearing he would expect more experience and sophistication than she had to offer. But she guessed he would be as dominant in bed as he was out of it, and hoped that the love she felt and the desire to please him would be enough.

'Come here,' he said softly. She went gladly and trustingly into his embrace. He put his hands lightly on her waist and the touch of his fingers seared her flesh through the silk of her dress, and it was she who moved to bridge the slight gap between them.

He kissed her then; gently at first, then with increasing urgency. His arms tightened around her and he strained her to him, his tongue exploring and tantalizing the inner sweetness of her mouth.

Chrissie's senses reeled and she responded hungrily, feeling the hardness of his body against hers and exulting in it, acutely aware of an answering hot ache of desire deep within her.

His hands moved to caress her shoulders, slipping down the thin straps of her dress and easing it away. With practised ease, his fingers found the zipper and tugged until the dress fell to her feet, leaving her naked except for her skimpy briefs.

He quickly tossed aside his jacket and tie, and ripped off his shirt, then reached for her again. Chrissie gasped out loud when her swollen breasts brushed against the hair on his chest, and felt her nipples harden with need. She shuddered as his hands caressed and teased them, then, with his mouth still claiming hers, he swung her bodily off her feet and carried her to his bed.

He quickly rid himself of the rest of his clothes and paused to look down at her, his sapphire blue eyes glittering with desire as they devoured every inch of her.

'You are so beautiful,' he murmured, his hands gentle

as he caressed her, his touch expert and knowing as he slowly followed the contours of her body, bringing her to a peak of quivering response. Instinctively, she arched towards him, twining her arms around his neck to bring him closer.

He lay down beside her, still stroking her soft curves as he began kissing her, deeply and satisfyingly. Chrissie felt only gladness when he removed her briefs, the last barrier between them, and sighed in blissful anticipation when his fingers imitated the act of consummation, his touch sure and confident, knowing the secret needs and desire of her body better than she did herself. He brought her to a climax, content for now at least to watch the expression on her face and hear her ragged breathing and incoherent sounds of fulfilled passion.

Chrissie came back to reality slowly, and only then realized what he had done.

'I...you didn't...' she stammered.

'We have all night, sweetheart,' he told her huskily, already beginning a new assault on her senses, stroking and kissing, touching and tasting, until she felt the knot of desire begin to build again. She needed to know if she could make him feel as wonderful as he made her feel, and returned his caresses, then became bolder and knew a purely female triumph when he moaned his pleasure.

'I want you,' he groaned, and lifted himself over her. Chrissie instinctively moved to meet his thrust, unable to stop herself crying out as he entered her, deeply and strongly. He stifled her cry with his mouth and his hands moved beneath her buttocks to mould her even more closely to him.

Chrissie clung, arms and legs wrapped tightly around

him, undreamed of pleasure spiralling towards an ever greater delight, ever increasing peaks of ecstasy such as she had never known existed. Then she felt her entire body shudder with orgasm, felt his own climax deep within her as he cried out in exultation.

She lay, quiet and spent, utterly content, aware of her own rapid breathing and the heavy pounding of his heart next to her own. Then he eased his weight from her and lay beside her, cradling her to him. Wordlessly, he reached for the quilt and pulled it over them, wrapping them both in a cocoon of warmth.

Chrissie turned her face into his shoulder and hugged him fiercely, as if she could imprint herself on him for ever. Trent returned the embrace, holding her just as tightly, then he stretched out one arm to dim the light to a soft glow.

'Go to sleep,' he urged softly.

'I don't want to sleep,' Chrissie protested, but she was already succumbing. 'Wake me up soon,' she mumbled, stifling a yawn.

'Count on it,' he promised, dropping a kiss on her bare shoulder. Chrissie gave a sigh of mingled contentment and exhaustion and, within a few moments, her breathing became regular and even, her body soft and relaxed against his.

Trent didn't sleep: he gazed down at her in the half darkness and allowed himself the luxury of imagining how his life would be transformed if she stayed with him. He was sure she would, if he asked her, so he owed it to her to be strong enough for both of them and resist the almost overpowering temptation to ask.

He couldn't bear to make her as unhappy as he had made Francesca; to live through the gradual disintegra-

tion of another relationship, to see the growing dissatis-
faction with his long working hours, to watch her gaze
wistfully at other women's babies.

Chrissie was so young, she would be happier with
someone her own age, someone who had not been married
before and still bore the scars, someone who, far from
dreading the news of a pregnancy, would welcome it and
joyfully anticipate, with her, the birth of a child...

He shook his head to clear his brain: he had promised
them both one perfect night and he wasn't going to ruin
it with his own dark thoughts of her marrying another
man. He placed one hand possessively over her breast; it
was a light touch only, but, even in her sleep, the nipple
hardened beneath his palm.

Chrissie awoke as his mouth closed over the fullness of
her breast, his tongue warm and wet against the taut flesh.
She laced her fingers in his hair, holding his head to her
and feeling again the flame of need rise in her, demanding
satiation. She moved her hips against him in blatant invitation, but he pulled away slightly.

'Not yet, sweetheart,' he muttered thickly, and pushed
her gently back against the pillows. Chrissie gasped as his
mouth began to move tantalizingly slowly downwards,
from her breasts, over her ribs and to the flatness of her
stomach and then seeking the female core of her.

The expert touch of his tongue made her groan out loud,
and she dug her nails into his back as she felt herself
spiralling once more towards that peak of ecstasy where
time was suspended and nothing existed but such
exquisite pleasure that it was almost painful in its
intensity.

Trent drew back to watch her face, deriving as much
pleasure from her climax as she did. Or so he thought,

until she began imitating his actions, using her hands and mouth to give him the same wondrous delight. He was dimly aware that she lacked experience, but intuition served her well, he thought, before he almost stopped thinking at all.

Then, before he lost control, he moved swiftly and tipped her on to her back, his mouth seeking hers, hotly demanding as he plunged deeply into her. Chrissie opened herself to him, her lips soft and moist; she welcomed the plundering of his tongue and the urgent thrusts of his body.

Their lovemaking was even fiercer than before, as if the passion they had slaked earlier had risen, Phoenix-like, to burn ever brighter, needing an even greater fulfilment.

It was a long time before it was over and they lay together, sweat-slicked bodies entwined, hearts beating as one, until their quickened breathing gradually slowed, and this time, they both fell into a sleep of exhaustion.

Trent woke first, and was amazed to discover it was nine-thirty. He eased carefully away from Chrissie and left her sleeping while he showered and shaved. She stirred slightly when he returned to the bedroom to dress, but soon snuggled back down under the covers. He watched her for a moment, his heart full of longing for what he knew he couldn't have. He mouthed the words he couldn't say out loud – I love you – then quietly left the room.

A table lamp was still switched on in the hall from the night before and he reached under to flick the switch. As he did so, the glint of his wedding ring caught his eye and he stared at it. He had barely been aware of it for years, but he was acutely aware of it now. He yanked it off and tossed it into a small drawer.

Chrissie awoke to the delicious aroma of freshly-brewing coffee and she lay for a moment, savouring the memories of the night before. She felt tired and heavy-limbed, but gloriously so, and she stretched languidly.

'Good morning,' Trent smiled at her from the open doorway. He looked gorgeous, if overdressed, she thought wantonly, in chinos and open-necked blue shirt. She suddenly felt a little self-conscious in her nakedness. And her hair must look like a bird's nest.

'Good morning,' she echoed, a little shyly. Trent sensed her reserve.

'I'm cooking breakfast – what would you like?' he asked easily.

'Oh, whatever you're having will be fine,' she assured him. Goodness, he could cook, as well!

When he returned to the kitchen, she cast aside the quilt and scuttled into the bathroom. Her reflection in the mirror startled her; true, her hair was in total disarray, but the unusually full mouth and sleepy, satisfied glow in her eyes told their own story. The story of a woman in love and, surely, a woman who was loved, even if only just a little, in return?

She heard the phone ring while she was still in the shower, but thought little of it. It was probably his mother, wanting a progress report! she thought, with a happy grin. As she dried off, she looked around for something to wear. She tried on Trent's dressing gown but, despite loving the faint scent of him on the material, quickly discarded it. Not sexy at all, not on her, anyway, although it probably was on him, she thought.

The lavender-blue party dress which she'd worn the night before was out of the question, so she settled for a clean bath towel, knotting it above her breasts, fluffed out her hair and sauntered off in search of Trent, food and coffee. Not necessarily in that order – she was starving!

'...They can't get away with that! They're under contract!' Trent was obviously still on the phone and she hesitated, not sure whether she should intrude on what was evidently a business call.

'I know it's Sunday, and I don't care if he is on the golf course,' Trent continued irritably. 'Get him on his mobile. I want to see both of you in my office, in one hour. We'll have to get this sorted today.' He slammed down the receiver and sighed heavily.

Chrissie glanced down at the towel, worn to seduce, and slowly returned to the bedroom. No longer hungry, no longer happy, she dressed in the skirt and sweater she had worn the day before.

'Chrissie...Oh, you are dressed,' he said, and sounded relieved, she thought dully, averting her gaze from him and feigning interest in the contents of her bag. 'I have...'

'I know; I heard,' she interrupted.

'I am sorry. I was going to drive you home...' he began, and Chrissie's head shot up as pain stabbed at her heart. So, he hadn't changed his mind about their only having one night together. Even before the phone call, he had planned her departure.

'Don't worry about me,' she interrupted again. 'I bought a return train ticket; there's no point in wasting it.' She couldn't quite keep the note of bitterness out of her voice, and Trent eyed her warily.

'Don't make this any harder than it already is,' he said quietly.

'Me? I'm the one making things difficult?' she asked incredulously. 'I don't understand you at all. Unless you were play-acting last night, we could be so happy...'

'You know I wasn't play-acting,' he said, hardly able to bear the pleading in her eyes and voice. But he was ending it now, for her own good if only she would realize that, and he deliberately hardened his voice.

'You *do* understand, Chrissie,' he continued grimly. 'I explained yesterday. I can't offer commitment; I was a lousy husband and I won't repeat the mistake. For your sake, as well as my own,' he added. Chrissie shook her head stubbornly.

'I don't accept you were a lousy husband,' she said. 'The wrong one for Francesca, maybe. But I'm not her! I'm nothing like her,' she went on, ignoring the inner voice warning her to never, ever criticise a dead wife. 'I'm not pining for a family living abroad, as she was. I work for a living, which she didn't. I'm not needy or clingy, and, most of all, I am not desperate to become a brood mare. I…'

'That's enough,' Trent interrupted harshly.

'I haven't finished.' Chrissie was angry now. 'If I thought you were working too late at night, I wouldn't sit at home, crying about it.' She paused, then continued slowly, deliberately. 'I would come to your office, wearing a coat and nothing at all underneath it. Or perhaps just stockings and suspenders,' she added softly. 'Which would you prefer to have on your desk – me, or a stack of papers?' she challenged him. He couldn't answer. He sighed and raked his hand through his hair.

'This is getting us nowhere…'

'Which is precisely where you want us to be!' Chrissie said bitterly. 'I'm not asking for marriage or children. But…but why can't we be together?' she whispered.

'I'm too old for you, too jaded. You should be with someone your own age,' he said.

'Ben?' Chrissie taunted, and he flinched.

'No! Charles Hawksworth maybe. You loved him once.

And he loved you. He wanted to marry you.'

'We were just kids! Anyway, what makes you think that Charles would want your leavings?' she demanded bitterly.

Trent forced himself not to react. Couldn't she see this was killing him? 'I'm going to the office. If you've calmed down by the time I get back…'

'I won't be here when you get back,' Chrissie said, summoning up her pride and self-respect. 'There's no point, is there?' she challenged.

'Don't rush off. Have breakfast…' He came to a halt when she glared at him. 'I have an account with a local taxi firm – the number's by the phone…'

'I'm perfectly capable of getting across London by myself,' she said coolly.

'I'm sure you are.' He stared at her, saw the pain behind her anger and had to struggle hard not to pull her into his arms, and beg her to stay. 'I'll phone you…'

'Don't bother. Not unless you've decided to stop hiding behind Francesca's ghost!' Chrissie snapped, far too upset to be diplomatic. Trent's lips tightened.

'Goodbye, Chrissie.'

She heard the door slam behind him and bit down hard on her lower lip to stop herself from crying out, begging him to stay. Then, moving like an automaton, she searched for her shoes and even a jacket, before remembering she hadn't been wearing one. She certainly wasn't going to take the one he had bought her. The lavender dress was still on his bedroom floor, and she left it lying there; she would never be able to wear it again.

As she was about to leave, she spotted the second carrier bag containing the pink suede suit she hadn't noticed him buy. She fingered the soft suede, and some of her anger dissipated. That had been kind…or had he bought it as a pay-off? Thanks for a lovely evening, now here's a gift to take home…?

She kicked the bag viciously and left it lying on its side, the suit spilling out on to the carpet. He could keep his presents for someone else!

chapter thirteen

Chrissie's anger sustained her until she was on a train heading back to Farminster. Then, sitting huddled in a window seat, she stared out at the passing scene until it blurred before her eyes.

Tears began to trickle down her cheeks, slowly but persistently, then faster and faster until she could no longer wipe them away and stopped even trying. She sobbed out her heartbreak in front of a dozen passengers who, thankfully, pretended not to notice.

She had hoped she would feel better once she reached the sanctuary of her own home, but instead, the four walls seemed to close in on her, and the Sunday afternoon silence stretched out endlessly in front of her. On impulse, she phoned Dan Thomson and he, at last, seemed pleased to hear from her.

'What can I do for you, Chrissie?' he asked jovially.

'I thought I'd come back to work tomorrow, if that's OK with you?'

'You're not leaving Farminster, then?' he asked. Chrissie didn't reply to that. She needed to be occupied for however short a time she remained in the town. 'Of course you can come back. We'll iron out details of a new contract in the next few days. I meant what I said about a rise in salary and more responsibility,' he assured her.

'That's great,' Chrissie tried to sound as if she cared. 'I'll see you tomorrow.' She disconnected, then phoned Sally who, she hoped, would also be pleased to hear from her. She felt she needed all the friends and allies she could muster.

Sally was indeed delighted to hear she was returning to the office, although Chrissie neglected to tell her of the promised pay increase. It might never happen, anyway. Besides…

'Keep this to yourself, Sal, but I might not be staying very long. I'm seriously considering selling up and moving away,' she said.

'Where to?'

'No idea. Just away from here. So that I won't see Ben or Celia Fairfax, and won't keep hoping I might see Trent, or hear news of him…' She broke off. Amazingly, she still had some tears left to shed.

'Are you crying?' Sally demanded.

'No,' she sniffed.

'What's been happening? The last I heard, you were going out for dinner with Trent Fairfax on Friday night.'

'God, that was a lifetime ago.' Chrissie shuddered: she'd almost forgotten the pig in the White Hart car park. At least she'd got one thing right – Trent *had* been able to erase her memories of the assault. She didn't tell Sally about that, but gave the impression she'd been with Trent since Friday evening.

'He didn't lead me on, or lie to me. He was very clear about not wanting marriage or children, but I suppose I fooled myself into thinking he would change his mind, if only to the extent of having a relationship without commitment,' she finished sadly.

'So you did sleep with him?' Sally knew Chrissie must feel deeply for him if she had. She had something of a reputation for being an ice maiden.

'We didn't do much sleeping,' Chrissie tried to joke, but

choked on a sob instead.

'Have you really thought what it would be like to be a second wife?' Sally asked earnestly. 'From what I hear, it's hard enough when the guy's divorced and it must be a hundred times worse if he's widowed.'

'I'd risk it,' Chrissie said unhesitatingly.

'But what about his attitude to children? You don't want any now, but you probably will in a few years' time,' she pointed out.

'Not necessarily. Anyhow, he might change his mind. And I'm as healthy as a horse; there's no reason to believe I'd have problems like Francesca. I could make him happy, Sal, I know I could.'

Trent knew she could, too. And the knowledge was gnawing away at him. His senior staff, disgruntled at being summoned to his office on a Sunday, were grouped around his desk, but he wasn't listening to a word.

And the papers in his hand might have been written in Chinese for all the sense he could make of them. He could think only of Chrissie's taunting words – what sort of coat would she wear to cover her nakedness when she came here to seduce him away from his work? Fur, he hoped. Very non politically correct, but so were his thoughts. Or leather, perhaps? Or an outwardly sensible trench-coat, tightly belted at her tiny waist, but unbuttoned – to reveal tantalising glimpses of her shapely thigh with every step…

'Trent!'

'Huh?' He looked up uncomprehendingly, but heard the note of exasperation in his accountant's voice and guessed he had already repeated himself more than once. 'Sorry, gentleman, I can't concentrate on this now. I'll take the papers home and study them later.' He stood up in dismissal.

They exchanged looks of 'He got us in here on a Sunday – for this?' but nodded their agreement and gladly filed out of his office.

Left alone, Trent wandered across to the window and wearily leaned his head against it. He knew he had done the right thing in sending her away, so why did it hurt so much?

Chrissie settled back into the office routine as though she had never been away. The other members of staff greeted her as if she had been on holiday for a week instead of being sacked and then re-instated.

Only Sally and Reg Ford knew the whole story anyway, and they kept it to themselves, Sally out of loyalty and Reg because he feared for his own job after the mistake he had made over Chrissie.

Chrissie had gone for a coffee break when Annie, the junior receptionist, popped her head round the door.

'Someone to see you, Chrissie. Name of Fairfax,' she said, and was almost killed in the rush.

'Oh.' The disappointment was crushing. 'Hello, Celia,' she said dully.

'Hello, dear,' Celia scanned her face anxiously. 'I called at your cottage and your neighbour told me you would be here. It didn't go well, did it?'

'Have you spoken to him?' Chrissie parried the question. Besides, she wanted to know what Trent had said. But Celia shook her head.

'I've left several messages, but he hasn't got back to me. What happened, Chrissie?' she asked gently, feeling responsible for the girl's obvious unhappiness.

Chrissie shrugged.

'He sent me home,' she said baldly.

'I'm so sorry. I wouldn't have encouraged you to go, if I'd thought…' She broke off.

'Don't blame yourself. I probably handled it very badly. I certainly didn't help matters by saying Francesca was apparently a whinging little cow.'

'You didn't!' Celia gasped, a hand to her mouth. Chrissie nodded glumly.

'Not those exact words, but I definitely implied it,' she sighed.

'Well, she did seem to burst into tears at the slightest provocation,' Celia told her.

'I'm not sure I blame her – Trent can be very provoking,' Chrissie retorted, though with the faintest glimmer of a smile. Celia patted her hand, admiring her spirit.

'You'll win,' she said confidently. 'Don't make the mistake of thinking he's put her on a pedestal. I think he feels even more guilty about what happened because he knows the marriage wouldn't have lasted. Now, I can see you're busy,' she added, with a glance at an impatient couple waiting behind her. 'But will you come to dinner soon?' Chrissie hesitated.

'Can I call you in a few days?' she asked. She didn't feel up to answering more of Celia's questions. Maybe soon she would want to talk about Trent, but not yet. It was too raw a wound.

'Of course.' Celia hugged her briefly. 'If there's anything I can do…? No, I've done too much already, haven't I?' she sighed and went sadly on her way.

However, she wasn't quite finished. She phoned Trent once more, well, his answer-phone and, despite hating talking into machines, she reminded him of his stillborn sister, and also told him of the anxious time she and his father had experienced in the months before Ben was born, when they had feared another loss. She also told him he would be a fool not to grasp his chance of happiness. But Trent didn't respond to that phone call either.

For Chrissie, the days limped by, much as they had done before she had met Trent Fairfax, but she couldn't shake off her depression and loneliness. It was odd; she had always considered herself quite content with her lot, but she now knew she had been drifting aimlessly through life. It was time to go. She had accepted the increased offer on her house and, after she had repaid her mortgage, would have a considerable sum of money to help her start again somewhere new.

Charles Hawksworth arrived from Australia, sporting a deep tan, sun-streaked blond hair and an antipodean drawl. Chrissie was pleased to see him again; they enjoyed a drink together and laughed over old times. She accepted the invitation to his party, but mainly because she recalled James telling Trent he would send him an invitation, too. She had spoken to Celia and knew she was definitely going to attend, as was Ben, now out of hospital and causing mayhem in his wheelchair.

Chrissie splurged on a gold crochet mini-dress and knew she looked her best. Carefully applied make-up concealed the slight shadows caused by sleepless nights, and she had lost a little weight, which she felt suited her, making her seem taller and her legs even longer.

The Hawksworths had hired a fleet of taxis to ferry their guests to and from the party so that no-one need worry about drinking and driving but, as Chrissie stepped out of her cab, her heart skipped a beat at the sight of Trent's Mercedes. He was here!

So were hundreds of other people – half the county, seemingly – and she searched the crowd anxiously for a glimpse of him. She greeted her hosts and accepted a glass of champagne from a waiter, then continued her search. She spotted Ben holding court in his wheelchair and waved cheerily but didn't approach him. Annabel Harrington-Smyth was with him, and she didn't feel capable of dealing with the girl's snide remarks. Where was Trent? She wanted to scream with frustration. He must know she would be here, for she had told Celia, so he wouldn't have come unless he wanted to see her. Would he?

Charles Hawksworth noticed Trent walking alone through the conservatory and out towards the swimming pool, and went in pursuit.

'Hello, Charles,' Trent turned at his approach.

'G'day,' Charles grinned, and accepted Trent's outstretched hand.

'Does it feel good to be back?' Trent asked. 'How long are you staying?'

'That depends,' Charles shrugged. 'I'm trying to persuade someone to go back to Australia with me,' he explained. Trent stiffened.

'Who?' he asked, through clenched teeth.

'A girl I was in love with before I left England. As soon as I met her again, I knew nothing had changed,' he said dreamily.

'Chrissie Brennan?' Trent's hands were balled into fists. He had told himself – and Chrissie – that this would be the best thing that could happen to her, but the reality hurt a thousand times more than he had anticipated. 'Does she feel the same way?' he gritted out.

'Not yet. She's hung up on some older guy who's dumped her. He must be blind and insane if he doesn't want her, but hopefully his loss is my gain,' Charles said cheerfully. 'I'm trying to convince her she needs a fresh start in a new country. In fact, I'm going to propose to her tonight…'

'You do, and you're a dead man!' Trent snarled, and pushed past him.

Charles watched him go, then sauntered back to Ben.

'Sorted?' Ben asked. Charles nodded.

'I'd say so. I thought he was going to thump me!' He pointed to where Trent was forging a path through the crowd with all the ruthlessness of a shopaholic on the first day of Harrods' sale. 'There goes a man on a mission!' he laughed.

'Thank God for that. He's been even more unbearable than usual these past few weeks, and I need him to pay for a new Porsche!' Ben grinned up at his old friend.

Trent continued pushing his way through the mass of people. He had to find her. She was hurt, she might just say 'yes' to Hawksworth; be tempted to start a new life on the other side of the world…

'Chrissie!' He stared at her hungrily, momentarily rooted to the spot, then he grabbed her hand and pulled her in his wake as he tried to find somewhere private. He soon discovered that this was damn near impossible. How could one family know so many blasted people? Finally, he yanked open a side door which led out into the gardens, and drew her into the shade of a lilac tree.

'Please forgive me for hurting you,' he said urgently. 'Sending you away was the hardest thing I've ever done. But I thought it was the best thing for you.'

'It wasn't!' Chrissie finally found her voice. 'It was horrible…'

'I know; I've been so miserable without you. I can't eat, sleep or work. I love you, Chrissie, please don't accept Charles's proposal…'

'What?'

'I need you more than he does. And you don't love him, you love me… Don't you?' he asked, suddenly unsure. Had he hurt her too much for her to forgive him? Chrissie smiled and put her hand wonderingly on his cheek. He was here, solid and real, his wonderful sapphire eyes glittering with hope, passion and a hint of fear. All her unhappiness melted away and she slid her arms around his neck.

'Yes, I love you,' she murmured.

'Will you marry me? Please?'

'Oh, yes…!' He kissed her then, hard and bruising, his arms around her like bands of steel, until, as if realizing that she wasn't going to disappear, his touch gentled and the kiss became softer and deeper.

'You mustn't ever think being a second wife means you're second best,' he told her gruffly. 'I love you more than I ever loved her. Don't ever feel jealous.'

'How could I be jealous of someone you were in love with when I was still at primary school?' she teased.

'Ouch!' Trent winced. 'Unfortunately I *am* twelve years older than you. Do you mind?'

'The age difference has never occurred to me. Besides, guys my age are immature,' she shrugged dismissively.

'Mmm, you had to grow up quickly, didn't you, sweetheart? But you'll have a family again now. And, if you want to add to it, that's fine…'

'Children, you mean?' Chrissie was amazed by his

change of heart, and knew it was a measure of his love for her that he was prepared to overcome his fears about pregnancy and childbirth if that was what she wanted. 'I haven't thought much about it,' she said truthfully. 'It was always something I might do, but way into the future.'

'I'd like to have you all to myself for a while,' he admitted. 'But promise me you'll tell me when you feel ready for motherhood? Don't hide it from me because of my irrational fears.'

'I promise.'

'Good.' He kissed her again and held her close, enjoying the feeling of her seductive body pressed against his. 'Do you want to rejoin the party, and tell everyone we're getting married? Or shall we just slip away?'

'Slip away,' Chrissie said unhesitatingly, much to his delight.

'I love you,' he hugged her tightly, then took her hand and led her towards his car.

'Trent? What did you mean, about Charles proposing to me?' Chrissie asked, puzzled. 'He's already engaged. That's why he's back here – he brought his fiancée home as a surprise to meet his parents.'

'What?' Trent stared at her, then threw back his head and laughed. 'I must have got the wrong end of the stick,' he said, knowing he hadn't. He'd bet Ben was behind that charade. 'Remind me to send them a very expensive wedding present,' he said, still chuckling as he started up the car.

Celia didn't need psychic powers to guess what had happened when Trent and Chrissie strolled into her drawing room the following morning. Chrissie was dressed casually in jeans and a sweater, while Trent was wearing the dinner jacket of the night before, minus his tie and with several buttons missing off his shirt. He was badly in need of a shave and looked thoroughly disreputable. He also looked incredibly happy, with a lightness to his step his mother hadn't seen in years, and had sometimes despaired of ever seeing again.

'Oh,' she put a hand to her mouth and gazed from one happy face to the other, her eyes glistening with tears of joy. 'You…'

'We're getting married,' Trent told her, with a broad smile. 'As soon as possible.'

'Oh, I am so glad to hear that!' Celia rushed forwards and enveloped Chrissie in a tight hug. 'God bless you,' she whispered, for her ears only, before turning to her son and kissing his cheek. 'Congratulations!' she beamed, then became brisk. 'Will you let me help? There will be so much to do. Chrissie, I think you'd better move in here,' she decided happily.

'Oh, good,' Trent murmured, his eyes twinkling in anticipation.

'And you're barred from the house,' Celia told him firmly. He blinked.

'Barred?'

'Yes, it's not right for you and Chrissie to be under the same roof…'

'But we've…' he interrupted.

'Trent! I am your mother. There are certain things I would rather not know,' she said primly. 'In the absence of Chrissie's parents, it's my duty to ensure things are done properly.'

'I think I'd prefer to do them improperly,' Trent protested. Chrissie giggled.

'I daresay. You're still barred,' Celia told him.

'I wouldn't mind, but my kid brother is practically running his own harem not fifty yards from the house,' Trent grumbled. 'You don't complain about that.'

'I would if he were getting married,' Celia retorted. 'Now, Chrissie, have you thought of someone who can give you away? And bridesmaids, of course. I...'

'Excuse me,' Trent put in hastily, 'but I think I'd better go and square things with Ben.' He gave Chrissie a kiss and a hug and then went in search of his brother, hoping Ben's feelings for Chrissie were as superficial as he had always believed them to be.

He found Ben in his apartment, lying on the sofa with his injured leg propped up on cushions while he read the newspapers. Ben gave him a long look, then grinned.

'Dirty stop out,' he accused. 'It was nice of you to ensure Ma and I got home safely last night,' he added sarcastically. Trent looked momentarily abashed.

'Sorry, I completely forgot about you,' he confessed.

'I guessed that. And, since you look both blissfully happy and completely knackered, I can also guess that Chrissie is to be Mrs Fairfax after all?'

'Yes.' Trent felt he held an unfair advantage standing on two unbroken legs, and hunkered down so that his face was level with Ben's. 'Are you OK with that?' he asked quietly.

'Of course I am. I masterminded the whole thing,' he boasted. 'I knew you'd take the bait once I nicked Grandmother's ring for her.'

'Right.' Trent didn't believe a word of it, but pretended to. 'I owe you,' he said lightly.

'Will you pay for a new Porsche?' Ben was quick to seize the opportunity. Trent laughed.

'OK,' he agreed. 'But only on one condition – that you'll will be my best man?'

'Of course I will. It means I get first crack at the brides-maids,' Ben said cheerfully. 'This wheelchair is a real babe magnet,' he confided. 'And I promise not to lose the ring.'

'Great.' Trent decided to have a second ring tucked safely into his own pocket, just in case.

'How does Chrissie feel about having children?' Ben was suddenly serious.

'She doesn't want any yet. When she does, well,' Trent shrugged. 'I'll be worried sick about her, but I can deal with it. For her sake,' he added simply.

'And for yours. You'd make a terrific father,' Ben told him.

'You think so?' Trent was surprised.

'Yeah, well you've done a pretty good job on me!'

'I think the jury's still out on that one,' Trent said dryly. He got to his feet, anxious to get back to Chrissie.

'Trent?'

'Yes?' he turned.

'In case you were wondering… she wouldn't sleep with me. I never even got close,' Ben admitted. Trent smiled.

'I know. But thanks for telling me,' he said, appreci-ating the gesture.

When he returned to the main house, Celia was still in full flow, flitting from talking about bridal gowns, flowers, food and drink, and guests and back again to bridal gowns. Chrissie, tired after an almost sleepless night, and hovering somewhere above cloud nine, was barely taking in a word. Trent crossed over to her and perched on the arm of her chair.

'How would you like a quick trip to Gretna Green?' he murmured. She nodded her agreement, but Celia stopped in mid flow and glared at Trent.

'She would not like that at all,' she said firmly. Her fixed stare reminded him that, although he had been through this before, Chrissie had not. He inclined his head in acknowledgement of the rebuke: anyway, it hadn't really been a serious suggestion, he wouldn't deprive Chrissie of her wedding day.

'I was only kidding,' he assured them both.

'Good. Why don't you go and change, and have a shave?' Celia said next. 'You can drive us to London. Chrissie needs to start looking for a dress as soon as possible, and I'll need a new outfit,' she said, brightening at the very thought of shopping.

'That suits me,' Trent stood up. 'I need to get to the office. As from today, I'm delegating a large part of my workload.'

'I'm glad to hear it,' his mother approved. 'No more late nights at the office.'

'Well, maybe occasionally,' he drawled, and winked at Chrissie. She blushed: he had asked her if she would like a fur coat for her otherwise naked visits to lure him away from his desk. She wondered if she would ever dare follow through with her threat – or had it been a promise? With her luck, Trent would have left the building thirty seconds before she arrived and the only occupant of the office would be the caretaker. But then, she thought happily, her luck had just changed...for ever!

Romance at its best from Heartline Books™

We hope that you've enjoyed our latest selection of titles from Heartline Books. Over the coming months we will be offering you more new novels by both previously unpublished and experienced authors, containing stories with a dash of mystery, some which are tinged with humour and others high-lighting the passion and pain of love lost and rediscovered.

Our unique covers have been much admired and appreciated by our readers, capturing as they do evocative scenes such as a sleepy English town, an idyllic watermill and windsurfing off the coast of New Zealand.

Whatever the setting, you can be sure that our heroes and heroines will keep you enchanted and entertained for many hours.

Books we will be featuring in future months will include exciting stories, set in such glamorous locations as the steamy heat of the jungle, the sunshine coast of Australia and the dreaming spires of Oxford.

Why not tell all your friends and relatives about the exciting world of Heartline Books. They too can start a new romance with Heartline Books today by applying for their own, ABSOLUTELY FREE, copy of Natalie Fox's LOVE IS FOREVER.

To obtain their free book, they can:

- visit our website: www.heartlinebooks.com
- *or* telephone the Heartline Hotline on 0845 6000504
- *or* enter their details on the form below, tear it off and send it to:
  Heartline Books,
  FREEPOST LON 16243, Swindon, SN2 8LA

And, like you, they can discover the joys of subscribing to Heartline Books, including:

♥ A wide range of quality romantic fiction delivered to their door each month

♥ A monthly newsletter packed with special offers, competitions, celebrity interviews and other exciting features

Please send me my free copy of *Love is Forever*:

Name (IN BLOCK CAPITALS)

_____

Address (IN BLOCK CAPITALS)

_____

_____

_____

_____ Postcode _____

If you do not wish to receive selected offers
from other companies, please tick the box ☐

If we do not hear from you within the next ten days, we will be sending you four
exciting new romantic novels at a price of £3.99 each, plus £1 p&p. Thereafter,
each time you buy our books, we will send you a further pack of four titles.

Did you miss the first four exciting titles from Heartline Books?

SOUL WHISPERS by Julia Wild
BEGUILED by Kay Gregory
RED HOT LOVER by Lucy Merritt
THE WINDRUSH AFFAIRS by Maxine Barry

If you did, then please write to us at:
Heartline Books,
FREEPOST LON 16243, Swindon, SN2 8LA

And we will despatch these books to you.

Heartline Books...

Romance at its best™